The Enlightenment
of Katzuo Nakamatsu

AUGUSTO HIGA OSHIRO

Translated from the Spanish
and with an afterword by Jennifer Shyue

archipelago books

ISBN: 9781953861528
Library of Congress Cataloging-in-Publication Data available upon request.

Archipelago Books
232 3rd Street #A111
Brooklyn, NY 11215
www.archipelagobooks.org

Distributed by Penguin Random House
www.penguinrandomhouse.com

cover photo: Shomei Tomatsu
This work is made possible by the New York State Council on the Arts with the
support of the Office of the Governor and the New York State Legislature.
This publication was made possible with support from Lannan Foundation, the
Carl Lesnor Family Foundation, the National Endowment for the Arts,
and the New York City Department of Cultural Affairs.

Printed in the United States

The Enlightenment of Katzuo Nakamatsu

1

S TANDING ON A pebbled path in the Parque de la Exposición one
August evening, Katzuo Nakamatsu looked on at the sakuras blos-
soms. The branches of the small trees, which were scattered around
the park and laden with rosy flowers, glowed in the leaden light, filling
him with a private joy and, he believed, a secret spirituality. Children
played on the green lawn, couples chatted on wooden benches, pedestrians and families walked among the ancient fig trees and ceibos. He
took a deep contented breath, yes, the flowers were graceful and
lovely; then he walked toward the carp pond, shifting the angle of his
gaze, and still, the opaque light stayed the same, and the sakura
branches continued gleaming exquisitely. He smoked a cigarette, contemplating his perspective on the composite, the pond with green
water there, the perfumed sage here, surrounded by grass, creepers,

and the flushed sakuras, there was nothing to probe, no forehead wrinkles, no gesture of delight. Indeed, nothing foretold anything, not the lowery sky, not the people walking in the gardens, not the humdrum cooing of the pigeons, not the frogs moaning in the cisterns, until the strange moment when Nakamatsu began to feel burdened, the weight of consciousness, unseeing affliction. In the eternity of the instant, in a manner of speaking, the green of the afternoon flickered out, the park's babbling was erased, as if the world had taken flight, the pebbled paths disappeared, no serene gardens, or laughing families, or murmuring young couples, or ponds full of fish: the only thing in the air now was the sakura tree, its branches and its luminous flowers. And in that fragment of afternoon, from that imperturbable beauty, Nakamatsu noticed, sprang a death drive, a vicious feeling, like the sakura were transmitting extinction, a shattering, destruction. Facing this unusual, abnormal reflex, Katzuo managed to close his eyes, as if invaded by exhaustion, it all seemed like a dreadful illusion, abhorrent, and without knowing why he began to tremble, sweating, pallid, shaken to the core, unable to dislodge that feeling of death. He stood paralyzed on that pebbled path, face drained of color, eyes clouded over, breathing slowly, he focused inward, his hands wavered, and nevertheless, the horrendous feeling remained in his consciousness. He waited a moment, a sensible length of time, before opening his eyes, and this time he could make out, real and tangible, a crew of ekeko faces, marching through the grass under the sakuras, colorful chullos on their heads and leather pouches at their backs. Their hunchbacked figures bundled into suits and ties, they let out grunts and babbled in Quechua, their little mustaches accentuating their wax faces, they were like rag dolls, cartwheeling, tripping over each other, while the festive onlookers applauded, and cheered, and tossed coins. Uncouth, brutish, crude. He couldn't stand it. Aghast, Katzuo Naka-matsu fled, making his way on a paved path toward the gate that opened onto Avenida Garcilaso de la Vega, looking at no one, face forward, his head trembling, eyes wet with tears, alien to the street vendors selling ham sandwiches and ladling emollient as he plunged in among the vehicles and buildings on that central artery. He came to a stop on Paseo Colón, faltering, bewildered, unsure whether to cross the road full of minibuses and blaring horns, his body was dazed, in any case, the sensation of death had stayed in his consciousness, and an animal fear was hollowing out his belly, which was beset by a vio-lent churning, his throat was parched, he felt faint. Now, aimlessly, he moved through the dissolute streets, unrecognizable roads, past suffo-cating houses, impregnable stairways and doors, closed-up offices, and dark corridors, he had enough restraint left to keep himself from breaking into a run, and howling on all fours like a dog. His heart lashed. It was hard to breathe. There was a prickling in his legs. A blazing anguish, a brutal sun seemed to be burning his face, poaching his intestines, boiling on his back, sweat flooding, and the entirety of the street laid out before him, restaurants, vehicles, glass-paned doors, mere meters from him, looked iridescent and yellow, radiated a blinding light, in spite of the raw Lima winter sky. This is the solitude of hell, he said to himself, still on pins and needles, his skin burning, absorbing the heat, utterly lost, walking in no particular direction, guided by instinct. Only when he made landfall on Alfonso Ugarte did he recognize the wide avenue with its three arteries, he could see the silhouette of the roofs, a few balconies, the walls of the police station, the stony old houses, the hoarse puffing of the trucks, the provincials walking by, and for the umpteenth time he checked and confirmed the abyss of feeling alive, stricken, devastated. This is insanity, he noted with terror, and he could not fling himself down onto the avenue, could not screech, or bang against the wall, weeping over his misery, he told himself to calm down, continuing on his halting way through Breña's dense streets. With no tears or consolation, inhaling the unwholesome air, eyes wild, the frames of his glasses slipping down his nose, Katzuo, in that instant, felt a dreary cold, his feet were freezing, goosebumps lined his skin, and the coat he was in wasn't enough to keep him from trembling, it was as if he had shifted onto ice. It wasn't just in his head, the temperature had dropped, the dampness warping his bones, and the very streets were no longer visible, the pale light looking clotted, unreal, and beyond it no street corners existed, no businesses, residences, panels, lights, curbs: just emptiness. Katzuo idled outside of reality, body rigid, looking like a pale corpse, he was scarcely breathing, no longer groaning, he could feel his own dreadfulness, his stupidity, his fatigue. He told himself a second time, this is the solitude of cold, perhaps to confirm his own fate, but nothing mattered anymore, just death, his own irrefutable death. A glimmer of consciousness, and he found himself sitting on a bench, in Parque Manco Cápac across from the church on Avenida Iquitos, and there he saw the dark night, the deserted grass, parishioners and prostitutes circling the monument to Manco Cápac, the municipal hall on the corner, the uncertain walls of a school. He adjusted his coat, noted the dim light in the park, maybe three or four hours had passed, diminishing his torment; he decided to go back via Bausate y Meza, cross the boundary of Avenida Manco Cápac, and advance into the heart of La Victoria, via Luna Pizarro, Abtao, and Huamanga, Nakamatsu knew, these were the old hideaways he usually took one or the other of, since he recognized their colorful street corners, the furrowed concrete of the back patios, the drab liquor stores, uneven sidewalks, the streets with their posts and windows, the uproarious watering holes, the packed rooms, the scrunched-tight residences, the teenagers gathered in any old doorway. He inhaled the irreparable poor-neighborhood air, leaving behind the little windows in the houses, litter in the doors, the mechanics stationed there, the gaudy walls and fences, posters in drugstores, barbed-wire roofs, a newspaper stand, and the parked cars. This was the world he ought to leave behind, these streets so often trod, smelled, observed, bemoaned, that were being inexorably pulverized and erased before his eyes. No, never, he had never been able to join this reality, he had simply lived it indifferently, distantly, not getting involved, impassive, strange, marginal, he was after all the son of Japanese people, a *nisei*, almost a foreigner, and all those places, their people, were alien to him, they constituted those in his vicinity, the neutral zone where he deposited his gaze, and he was forbidden from joining, and being like them with their legs, their eyes, their arms. Of course, he often saw his friends, he could even hold a conversation, exchange opinions, gossip, questionable jokes, but never secrets, nor could he express his private feelings, because his Asiatic temperament prevented it, and his equanimity born of mistrust, frigidity, even disdain.

When he got to the small building where he lived, in the El Porvenir neighborhood, on extension La Mar block three, the listless Katzuo said to himself: the solitude of home. And indeed, after climbing the stairs to the second floor and entering the living room of his apartment, despondent, he began to walk in circles, looking at the pink walls, the dusty curtains over the window, quietly irritated, until he crumpled into his desk chair, in front of the bookcase, and lowered his head, his eyes fixed on the floor, breathing slowly, face still, whole body still, in a posture of helplessness. Nakamatsu didn't need to explode into complaints, recriminations, that wasn't his style, his shoulders sunken, brought low, he let his consciousness stir, with no illusions, much less hope. He was fifty-eight, depleted, old, death was approaching indifferently, he couldn't deny it, and because of some lack of foresight, perverse destiny or chance, his demise had been revealed to him, and he, impotent, ought to accept his lot without bitterness; when faced with that which could not be repaired, he found confrontation impossible. Perhaps yes, maybe no, it was plausible that fatalism, that old ancestral sediment, had been rejuvenated in his person, compelling him to passivity, non-resistance, to not violate the order of things, accept the dark plans for his death. That was how he understood it. In the larger cosmic equilibrium, a minute substance expired, reached its end, he, and life's infinite other forms, reappeared vigorous, lush, verdant, through nature's tumultuous transformations. As such, Katzuo Nakamatsu was required to submit; in his misfortune he worried about the shape his death would take: a car accident? a sudden heart attack? a murderous hand? He didn't know, and couldn't imagine, withdrawn into his serene contemplation, the unlit room, sprawled in his chair, in front of the bookcase, his head still, his neck, his feet, his shoulders, static, inert, focusing inward, the barest of gleams in his eyes behind the thick frames of his glasses.

2

THAT MONDAY HE woke up feeling listless, Katzuo Nakamatsu did, and starting at seven he drank several cups of coffee, feeling no real desire to take up his duties as a professor. Perhaps he still felt irritated, clogged with resentment, shriveled into himself, in any case, he paced in circles around the living room of his apartment, hands on his back, past the bedroom and the kitchen that opened onto the air shaft in the center of the building. In his rambling monologue addressed to imaginary interlocutors, nothing had happened, he tried to convince himself to keep living like before, like always, like every day, despite his premonitions, his fear, his pessimistic instincts, nothing mattered anymore, and if death must come for him, there was no escaping it, he told himself, he had to confront it lucidly, with open eyes, in all its inevitable determination. For the most part, he was a reserved man, orderly, averse to improvisation, and in the march of the years, he had acquired habits and attachments he found impossible to give up, even his walks, his outings, and his labyrinthine meanderings happened on known territory, his very existence splintered into settings he had traversed thousands of times, navigating known waters, as if the world were nothing more than a reiteration of itself. In some ways, he mused, those feelings, his inclinations, his joys, his minimal convictions were obliged to stay unchanged, absolutely eternal, just like his stony face, lean figure, vacillating gait, all his irrefutable gestures and compulsions.

And so, around noon, Katzuo Nakamatsu slowly showered, changed out of his house clothes, and relocated to the Terukinas' little restaurant on block 12 of Bausate y Meza, since he was craving *yushime*, an Okinawan soup that would bring back the flavors of his bygone childhood, now that his consciousness was full of indecipherable voices. Sitting in his chair, after greetings and a cordial exchange, he conversed with Juanita Terukina, the youngest sister, and soon the conversation turned down the old paths of the '50s, the children's games, the streets yellow with afternoon sun, the former Porvenir movie theater, and the various families that had scattered or been snuffed out, Japanese families among them. In the opaque light of the main room, images appeared in a torrent, of the Tairas, the Arakaki brothers, gruff Takeo Nakama, beautiful Margarita Matsuda and her chicken shop, the dazzling Alejandro Honda, and a flood of others Katzuo Nakamatsu conjured up against the backdrop of Juanita's placid voice. As if the walls, the warm surroundings where they found themselves, were the same aquamarine color they had been fifty years ago, still the same roof and accumulated smell, so too the smiles and dedication of the Terukinas, absolutely nothing had changed, not a shred, not a stroke, except the cabinets and the wood of the table showed signs of wear, traces of blur, and were no longer as fresh as in times past. It was a fragile moment, and that precarious instant was abruptly shattered by the explosion of bullets in the street. In the tumult they heard shouting, the blaring horns of the combis, a commotion, and so they went to the door, and saw some boys running down the gridlocked street, and then the crowd milling on the corner of Parinacochas. "He was killed right over there," exclaimed several people on the sidewalk, a few faces appeared in the windows, a mob of youngsters whorled around the billiards hall, other people clustered near the pharmacy. A neighbor came over, and said:

"It was a vendor in Gamarra, some gangsters tried to rob him, he fought back, took out a gun, and killed one of them; the others ran away."

And now, the scrupulous Katzuo Nakamatsu observed the impossible avenue, the figures crammed together, people's silhouettes, and felt like he was returning to unseeing reality, the everyday one engraved on scraps, on dross, on trash. Hands in his pockets, forehead stern and shoulders disdainful, he said goodbye to Juanita Terukina, and made his halting way down Bausate y Meza, dodging people, not excusing himself, oblivious to the grumbles, the outrage and the protests of the women he passed. He arrived at the corner of Parinacochas, and through the mob and the bottlenecked cars, saw the body lying in the street, a young man with a chicha lover's face, wearing shirtsleeves, sneakers, and blue jeans. They had covered him with newspaper, but nevertheless, the breeze made the paper flap, and the astonished eyes would come into view, the corner of the pursed lips, the violent chin, and the unruly blood on the black ground. In the coruscating light, Katzuo thought: *And for you the dog does not cry; / And for you no mother howls*, in any case, it was a resigned spectacle; the bullet had wrecked the boy's chest, and he could no longer breathe, or feel, or hear, or blink, collapsed there, lifeless, inert, and inoffensive, as if death had acquired the splendor of all that beauty collected. For a moment, Nakamatsu was captivated by the impassive flesh, perhaps he felt moved, it's also possible he stayed surly, distant; then he retraced his steps, shrugged his shoulders, crossed through the throng of people, feeling no pity, seeing no recourse, at the end of the day, the boy wasn't one of his dead or in his likeness, nor the extension of his body, nor of his blood, his eyes, his race. Perhaps he wasn't even a citizen; the old solitary wolf, burrowed into himself, returned to his path on Parinacochas, walking between the glassworks and the auto

13

repair shops, inhaling the foul grease fumes, sidestepping the posts swathed in cables, and peeping through the wretched windows of the housing blocks. Rounding the corner onto 28 de Julio, once again he joined up with the wide columns of vehicles, the frenetic microbuses, the avenue stamped with gray structures, the furniture stores, the hotels, the small markets, and then he felt the desire to cover his ears, hide his face, walk like an invalid, body lurching, without rhyme or reason, thinking about nothing, mind blank, not breathing. On the corner of Lucanas, in front of the gas station, he ran into Don Paco Mármol, a solicitous electricity company retiree, indefatigable reader on the weapons of the Second World War, humming Tchaikovsky's "Capriccio Italien" and waiting for the combi to Breña. They greeted each other unsurprised, sniffing around each other as each peered into the other's eyes; in the sinewy afternoon air they conversed about municipal neglect, the proliferation of youth gangs, and the corruption of the politicians; after a pause, without knowing why, suddenly, overcome by his doubts, Katzuo inquired:

"How could one kill oneself quickly and painlessly?"

Instantly, beaming, Paco Mármol grasped the question and answered without batting an eye:

"Gunshot to the temple."

Nakamatsu pressed: "How?"

"A Beretta 21, here on the right."

~

And he put a finger on the other man's parietal bone. Katzuo Nakamatsu absorbed the impact, he seemed displeased, nevertheless he looked up at the melancholy sky, the ramshackle trees, the horizon with no future, then, drawing strength out of his intestines, abrupt, like it was nothing, he reached his hand out to Paco Mármol's shoulder, gave him a few expectant claps on the back, and the two of them began to laugh uproariously, magnificently. Later, with the same discordant spirit, his conscience in a jumble, Katzuo continued on his way down Lucanas, listless, hunched, a bittersweetness in his mouth, with that measured gait, and the nostalgia of his repetitions, the thousands of times he'd traversed this dingy street, with its warped hovels, to get to the house on García Naranjo of Masao Uchida, an old schoolmate.

On the second floor, in the property's comfortable little living room, they sat side by side solving the crossword at the table, listening to the radio, talking about football, commenting on the pride of poor households on display in the criollo waltzes "De vuelta al barrio" and "Juanita." Masao Uchida sang them in the style of the streets, intensely and with sentimental flourishes, as Barrios Altos had been his stomping grounds as a boy, where he had learned how to feel, at the many cantina parties, a guitar held close. Now, he was retired from all activity, forced to shutter the bodega he'd once presided over on the ground floor, since the drug addicts and constant robberies had scared

15

off the customers. He lived quietly with his wife Kuni-*chan* off of the remittances their children sent from Japan; and then between reminiscences, chess matches, smoking, coffee, lewd jokes, it was eight in the evening. Katzuo Nakamatsu excused himself, citing exhaustion, and before retiring to his home, his voice emotionless, apathetic perhaps, his gaze inert, he asked to borrow the Star pistol, since there were far too many delinquents in the darkness of the streets. With no roughness, as was always true in adverse circumstances, Masao Uchida understood the situation exactly, and silently, with no fuss, he looked in the drawers of the cupboard. Then he loaded and cocked the Star with dispassionate hands, detached from it all, and handed it over, fully aware of what he was doing. Nakamatsu thanked him, relieved from the bottom of his heart.

3

T HE SEA WAS everything: the scent in the air, hidden desires, the morning's secret, its impermissible force, the fury of what was incomprehensible. For several days in a row, Katzuo Nakamatsu went down to the beach of the Costa Verde, strolling along the shore, since that clear space allowed his feelings to expand. It felt like a liquid mirror, a friendly spirit with whom to murmur incantations about his doubts, amid the breeze, the eternal waters, the winter fog, and the damp sand. He saw surfers, encountered the sporadic person fishing from the crags, some vagrant kids, then silence, and a leaden sky, armored and reflecting no light. Bundled in his green coat and wearing gloves, his glasses sliding down his nose, Nakamatsu returned again and again to the scenes of his childhood, his parents and relatives, the youthful episodes of inebriation, the world demolished by the arrival of the barbarians, the few friends he still had left. These were his memories of those days and his own departure from them, and as always he found no illusions, nor life rafts, the boat sank between his fingers, and all that there was around him was the haze, the smell of marine life in the shoals, ghostly dampness, the silhouette of the cliffs, and the ash-colored cars on the roadway. He was afraid of being shut into a vicious cycle, with no sense of north, no overcoat, no confidence, unease in his guts, and the hard nights of insomnia, bodily deterioration, Nakamatsu sensed it all, and perhaps all his sapience could do was extend his agonizing, draw him a breath, and harbor him in the dark night of his soul. He recited: "I am not the Other / I can tell you of nothing but myself / But who am I among what I am not? / Where could my fate go?" He inhaled, smiled briefly, distracted himself with the seagulls on the jetty, tilting his head, he closed his eyes, in difficult moments his rationality couldn't do much for him, as instinctive as this rescue device was, it too could turn into a fish bone in the throat, and every thought, every interpretation of his life, sank him further into defeat, into the closing off of paths, into vapid nothingness. Again he muttered, taking pleasure in the words: "Hope is a hard thing, / A human intestine, / Something to be hung from, how I don't know, / From the Soul, / Hangs like the body, / Hangs like its own nothing." He thought about Martín Adán, the afflicted poet, and felt that he was a spiritual brother, a twin consciousness in the storm, yes, a man raving at the margins, walled off from the world, majestic and destitute. Once, in his youth, Katzuo had seen Martín Adán alcoholic in the streets of el centro, during one of the periods he spent in a mental hospital, entrenched in his I, proclaiming his monologue for nobody, he had ended his days in the asylum, with a reputation for poetry, naturally, listening to his scandalous music. But that music was his very self, and years before *La mano desasida*, already beyond pain, guilt, and torment, Martín Adán had reached the other side of human wretchedness; utterly alone, with no fear of deaths, he was him, in his quiet poetry, which said nothing, pure tautology.

In the distance glided a barge gone astray. Nakamatsu felt that the gray had become denser, like sea vapor had coated the salt in the wind; walking with his hands in his pockets, he ended up at Agua Dulce beach by three in the afternoon. He found himself on the path by the cliffs, and emerging onto the embankment, he walked past the park and ate lunch at a restaurant on Avenida Chorrillos. Pacified, he wanted to think about nothing, he let his mind go blank, breathing deeply, as he always did, focusing on emptiness; outside the people were moving by on the street, the color of the air, no premonitions, no bitterness, a few shrubs, benches, and young people wandering around. He had reached, then, the normal temperature of his walks, heartbeat stable, consistency of the body, that good old bag of bones furnished, in this instant at least, a sense of well-being. For the rest of the afternoon, and even into the night, that balance remained, and so he was able to watch TV, and afterward he slept soundly.

The next day brought an overcast but refreshing morning, nothing to complain about, as he told himself, and as always he went on his way to the university; by eight he was on La Mar, and he made his way to the pharmacy to take his Xanax. Afterward, he got on a microbus on 28 de Julio, a ramshackle vehicle filled to the brim, but he didn't have much trouble settling into the aisle, among the fickle sardine-packed passengers. Through the window he could see the neighborhoods' disarray, the jam of traffic lights and car horns, countless people in the streets: scowling insolent men, bumbling women, street vendors in shirtsleeves. As they entered Breña, still in his spot in the aisle, over the breathing of the passengers, Nakamatsu felt an uncomfortable jolt; from the back of the bus someone was observing him, obsessive, mocking. Their eyes were fixed on the back of his neck, like a ludicrous animal, a wax figure, whose breath was devouring his back, leaving him with an impression of coldness. All the same, he did not turn his head, he didn't want to know who it was, he felt like he was melting into salt, burrowed into himself, withstood the blow; gritting his teeth, tensing his body, he pushed the discomfort out of his mind. Right away, spurred only by this moment of imbalance, he had the sensation that animals were springing from his consciousness; roaring pests, fierce dwarves and diluvian snakes knotted in his intestines. He had to tell himself to calm down, breathe in deep, silently count to a hundred, exhale slowly, not rust over, stay undaunted, and like always, freeze his posture, his face set, eyes distant, skin indifferent, impassive surface. He weathered the storm, and when he arrived at his stop, he carefully exited the microbus, with his head high, his arms and legs wide, walking down Avenida Universitaria, to the steady beat of his reptile feet, briefcase in hand; abstract, he entered the university through one of the side gates alongside a gaggle of students.

For him, the irreproachable, reliable professor, the campus was a theater full of background actors, the same ones as always, as if they were following a scenographic ritual, the neatly aligned patches of grass, the blocks of identical classrooms, the dense complex of administrative buildings with their sidewalks, and windows, and passages. And so he made his way to his office in the professors' section, and then he presented himself at the department office to submit the medical certificate excusing his absence of the past few days. There, he found some colleagues and students consulting the bibliographic index, as the secretary handed him a sealed envelope with his name on it; and he, Katzuo, opened it and began to read, seeing as it was a resolution from the academic rectorate. As he read, his face took on a look of confusion; blinking, breathing hard, he registered that he was being sent, unceremoniously, into retirement because of his age. Stunned, his body quaking, he didn't know how to process the news, it seemed like a joke, retirement, he said or thought, in any case nobody heard him, nor did they see him standing there, unscathed, uncomprehending, with a wounded air and a piece of paper in his hand. Perhaps he silently wept, or muttered curses; whatever it was, Nakamatsu closed his eyes, and felt that his body was being consumed by a flush, an icy fire in his belly. Then everything dissolved into darkness, suffocating circles pricking his head, an increasingly confused haze, warped voices, violent colors, unusual sounds emerging from dreamlike depths. When he returned to reality, Katzuo was in the courtyard, in front of a flower bed, surrounded by professors and students; between the security guards and employees, they had removed him forcefully from the dean's office. There he found out he had already been replaced in his courses, his students were no longer his students, and he had to hand his office over to the respective authorities. Friends and colleagues tried to calm him, they brought him to the university cafeteria and gave him chamomile water; at the end of the day the resolution was illegal, he could demand his rights before the supervisory body, they would advocate for him with the authorities. Then they took their leave, and, alone at one of the tables, amid the hubbub of people eating and the flow of the masses of students, Katzuo Nakamatsu took three hours to wrap his head around his situation, after taking Xanax, smoking several cigarettes, and drinking six cups of tea.

~

To clear his mind, he moved through the central building, and simply strolled through the little gardens, the track, and facilities, like a farewell ceremony, over there were the auditorium and the engineering schools. Near the library he started feeling nauseous, behind his back he heard mocking giggles, blustery talk, and insults, his own colleagues tossing out little remarks on the sly. Everyone knew, a resolution like this one couldn't have been finalized without the knowledge and initiative of the department head and other administrative bodies. A few boys were practicing in the gymnasium, he glimpsed some games of chess, the movement of couples on their way to a copse of trees via intricate little lanes. Yes, it was true, he could file an appeal, but processing the complaint and the accompanying quagmire could take months, or even years, he didn't know, and he didn't have support at the decision-making level, he'd always been on the margins of the professor cliques.

And so he left through the main gate and walked down Avenida Universitaria with no destination in mind, under the chilly mantle of the cloud-covered sky, holding his professor's briefcase. Something was draining out from between his fingers, time perhaps, or part of his life; he didn't quite understand, but once again death settled between his eyes, with its gloomy retinue. And in the midst of his distress, he wanted to breathe, to stir, persist in his little joys, without tears, without the aches, perhaps even until he was wheezing. He turned onto sinuous Avenida Bolívar in Pueblo Libre, a street he had gone down thousands of times, and without heaviness he understood that the trees, the road shoulder, the cracked corners with their houses and gardens, the Stella Maris clinic, had nothing to say to him, like they were lifeless, as if he had always been a passenger in the fog. After sixty minutes of walking, he had arrived on Brasil, and skirting the supermarket, lingerie shops, video stores, opticians, and fairgrounds, he decided to go to Parroquia San José, where he could sit sheltered under the church's slim stonework towers, and the delicate dome, and the little canopy. It was as if he felt in need of heavenly protection, *tariki*, the grace of assistance, since he needed to alleviate the floundering feeling, to assuage the helplessness. He focused on the altar, the cornices, the diminutive arches, and the deep ceiling, with its stained-glass silence, crystal chandeliers, paintings of the Passion, and space open to light. Overwhelmed by the stillness, he murmured his prayers to the Virgin Mary, closing his eyes, he quietly bowed his head and stretched his legs onto one of the benches, at this time of day there weren't many parishioners around. He was not resigned to fate, and those crucifixes, the pale gleam of those images and confessionals remained undisturbed, floating in tranquility, in the illusion of hope, as he asked himself what he had done with his life, how much at fault he was if he felt undone, unsociable, and reality itself continued to be a no man's land.

~

Once he was finished praying, Nakamatsu left the church, and went into the reserve courtyard, and once again he looked at the elegant lines of the towers, and noticed the whimsy that lifted them into the sky. He wanted, he needed, the balance, the heavy light of dusk and the pigeons on the sidewalk, and so he sat down on one of the benches in the park, to look at the combinations of nearby houses, the color of the walls. Shortly thereafter, he began to amuse himself by spying on a group of teenagers in the grass, skidding by after a ball. Katzuo looked at them and saw them brimming over, outrageous, with their pitted skin, their narrow faces; they looked so virile, running and shouting, with their chests bunched into shirts, and those manes of hair falling over their faces. It was his old nosy habit, marveling at their plump flesh and those boyish impulses, at what was no longer his to savor; those vigorous games, the endless hurtling around. He felt the impotence of his big old capitulating body, which would not stop oozing odors, dreary on a park bench. How long did he sit there paralyzed, with tears in his eyes, yearning for what was no longer possible for him? As evening fell, Nakamatsu observed himself hovering around the malls and businesses of Jesús María, asking after beauty, the weather, his stomach ulcer, and the slowness of his feet in the depths of the dark sky. Surrounded by a murmuring crowd, he posed an empty question to himself: why had he never loved, and why had nobody ever loved him? On Arnaldo Márquez he climbed into a taxi that took him to his house in La Victoria.

~

Nevertheless, after bathing and having coffee, eating fruit, and changing his clothes, he sat reluctantly down at his desk, and wrote down his impressions from the day: his shameful expulsion from the university. Perhaps, he said to himself, he would speak to a lawyer to keep the case open. After an hour, he turned on the TV, and started pacing around the living room, the bedroom, and the kitchen, hands behind his back. He breathed in deeply, thinking about nothing, observing the TV, rinsing glasses and plates, scrubbing a brush over the furniture; out of distraction or perhaps weakness he examined the spacious shelves of books, and understood that his projects were wisping into air. There was his study of Martin Adán, unfinished, the texts full of annotations, he was investigating a reasonable reading of his poems. Another stack was made up of his incomplete novels and stories, written in different periods, and none of them edited, likely due to laziness. In another crowded corner rested another dream, a biographical recounting of the lives of Japanese families located in Huaral and Lima, with recorded interviews as its source. Flipping through the yellowed pages, he recalled his efforts to reduce the interviews down into monographs that would include old photos and family trees, with anecdotes and detailed information spanning forty years. At some point Katzuo Nakamatsu had discerned that even his gait, his mental and physical composition, his hesitation to identify with other people, his neuralgic apathy, his pantheism, his penchant for nature, were rooted in that old foundation, in a time and space, that is, his Japanese being. All the same, after taking a hard look at himself, he vacillated in indecision; perhaps he felt this innate Japanese tropism from a distance, history and life's vicissitudes dissolving his paternal inheritance, leaving nothing but obscure tendencies and islets in his unconscious. In any case, beneath the bitter taste of doubt, the insuperable fact of existence was enough for Katzuo, he didn't need nationalism or the intrusion of customs, what he knew for certain was that he was living; everything else bordered on the metaphysical.

The Japanese people who were so familiar to him, his own unruly and inexpressive parents, had fought ruthlessly, facing up to hatred and rancor born of their being foreigners who never settled in. Because nothing disturbed them, they preserved even their ethos, and their uncontaminated race, their habits, their haughtiness, the din of their struggle, their notions of brotherhood, the ambiguity, and their indeterminate place at the margins of the country's whites, cholos, and mestizos. Nevertheless, they had died with a reputation for ferociousness and tenacity, and were reforged in their children, the *niseis* like Katzuo Nakamatsu, mercilessly uprooted, who even at the end of their years, after senseless experiences and moral defeats, in old age, still asked themselves: Why did our hides, our Japanese eyes, our bodily humors provoke such suspicion and rejection? Why were we

racist, coarse, why did we break our backs like cholos? All the per-
plexities, the resentments, the personal pitfalls left dark Nakamatsu
tattered, and still they pressed on, pushing him to the edge of a mental
jumble now that his untimely lot or whatever it was had set a snare in
his path, and was sliding him to the brink of suicide.

4

O NE SUNDAY MORNING, just as he had planned, Katzuo Nakamatsu made his way to El Ángel cemetery. According to what
he'd learned as a child, he had to make reconciliations with his dead,
and sort out that intimate part of his conscience; the visit would also
be a serene farewell ritual. At ten in the morning, he plunged as if
into a beloved territory, traversing the working-class part of Bausate y
Meza, its boys in doorways and at the curb. On the corner with Luci-
nas, next to a post: a parked car, radio on full blast, beer bottles strewn
on the ground. Nothing but the chipped walls, the gray awnings, the
bookstore or newspaper stand, the mattress men and scrap merchants
on Parinacochas, the nicked cornices, the seepage from the businesses
with their horrible patios, and the same old smells of boiled food. He
greeted a neighbor with his usual pallid surliness, amid the customary

crush of vehicles, vendors on their tricycle carts, vagrant recyclers with their sacks, and crowd of stands and orange sellers on Giribaldi. Huánuco was where the lowlifes prowled, nevertheless he was able to clamber onto a microbus, and with no heaviness, maneuvering around potholes and up the twisting main artery, the vehicle set off toward Grau. The lukewarm sun was heating up the streets, flea markets and the snarl of power lines coming in and out of view, when Katzuo found himself thinking about Keiko, his wife who had been dead for twenty-five years. He recalled her in the phosphorescence of Calle Albaquitas and Calle Capón in the Mercado Central, side by side with the Gushiken sisters as she worked in a Japanese-owned crockery store. There she was smiling, ordinary Keiko. Uneasy Keiko crossing Mesa Redonda. Indulgent Keiko at home in El Porvenir, attentive, sensible as she did the household chores. Nakamatsu conjured her up surrounded by Támi-*chan* and Shiyo at the Agaríes' restaurant, with the Okura family and Susana Kishimoto at La Unión stadium at the Japanese club, or at an *oshōgatsu* party on new year's, at the Kuniyoshis' chicken restaurant, since for Keiko, in the prime of her youth, there was no greater joy than getting together with her friends. This was how Nakamatsu liked to remember her, in those idealized happy times, among smiles that lingered, free of bitter shadows and winding conflict, even though they were so unlike each other.

When he got to the little plaza in front of the cemetery, he went past the shabby children and fritanga carts and bought flowers from one of the stands. When all was said and done, time went by in its meek way, reflections of pale light yellowing his surroundings, and visitors bounded across the pavement past the gates of El Ángel, then dispersed down the narrow cement lanes, passing the gloomy chapel and the snarled little gardens. There they were, the mausoleums, upright tombstones, the headstones in the lawn, the pigeons in the air, beds of canna lilies and pansies, and, vertical in the vast flatness, the barracks of the dead. And nevertheless, the smell of the cypresses and the proliferating paths returned to him once again the image of Keiko: petite, short hair, her face open and prone to smiles, enthusiasm her only personality trait. At least that was how it was when they got married at the Okinawan hall in Barrios Altos, with a banquet and traditional dancing. By then, the peaceable Katzuo had already become an instructor at the university. They were poor, worked painstakingly, and enjoyed themselves at the *nisei* carnivals, and he seemed untouchable in his detachment, and wrote cultural reviews for magazines and delighted in oral histories of Quechua mythology. Nakamatsu always knew: an arrangement of polar opposites, with no children, him introverted, Keiko enterprising, operating little businesses selling tempura and Japanese snacks in Chinatown on Calle Capón. She was an unabashed fighter, a realist, courteous, and then there was Katzuo, the thinker, intellectual, vacillating between the *nisei* world of his origins and the criollo world, like he belonged to nobody. Keiko would

31

open her eyes and rush forward, adaptable, unhurried, securing clients, offering beautician services. Katzuo closed his eyes, divided, ashamed of his foreignness, his head filling with illusions, impassive, teaching his classes, tolerating his racial fracturing without anguish. It was an eternal struggle between dexterous and practical Keiko, her sweetness and endearing talents; and the somber theorist, timorous spectator, Katzuo, blindfolded, maneuvering around cliffs, abysses, pests and snakes, walking on air with his fictions, unhearing, unseeing, unspeaking; absurd, perhaps, dragged forward by inertia. The precarious balance collapsed when Keiko died suddenly; then Katzuo closed into himself, and stopped visiting the Japanese community, lost the *nisei* friends who had been kin to him, and felt like more of an outsider than ever among all the upstart mestizos and crass andinos.

Absorbed in his thoughts, Nakamatsu wandered among the sepulchral structures, as he had done many times on his neurasthenic walks, monitoring the same patches of grass, until he identified the San Rafael block, the first on his route, where his mother Tamae, who died in November of 1981, lay buried. He cleaned off the marble, filled the vase with water, quietly tucked in his flowers, and, arms at his sides, bowed his head. With no showiness or frivolity, Katzuo complied with the customs of his childhood, observing the simple ritual, no pressing needs other than making peace with the universe of his dead. After finishing the ceremony with an unspoken farewell, he headed for the San Noberto division, twenty-five meters to the west, and repeated the exercise at the niche of his father, Zentaró, who passed in October of 1967. He felt no desire to reminisce about that belligerent, authoritarian old man, who came to Peru in 1918, from Yokohama, a poor immigrant, on the cargo ship Anyo Maru alongside two hundred and forty of his fellows, on their way to the haciendas in Cañete, according to the legend he heard as a child. Those bloodied and unsociable Japanese men, inert, shaped an alluvial land and retreated into untameability, the echoes and reflections of which arrived in bursts, the land bereft of familial conversations, the men of interest to no one, no melancholy for the past. After a while, around noon, Nakamatsu made his way to the outer edge of the cemetery, leaving behind the willows and eucalyptuses, the pavement, the gardens full of mallow and sunflowers, a small pond, docile balustrades; and amid the buzzing insects, he located the San Atanasio division, the last phase of his muted ceremony, the final resting place of his wife Keiko, who died in October of 1978, so he could repeat the ceremonial offerings. There was no hint of angst, or even apprehension; there lay the stubborn Keiko, thirty-nine, victim of cancer, untouched, unconquered, frolicking without a care, beyond spite and family resentments, free of torture, of sicknesses of the body. Keiko was happy, immensely blessed, Katzuo was sure of it, he simply placed his flowers and, smiling, bowed his head, thinking, *Death will come with your eyes*. And with that, he finished the ceremony, his farewell to his dead relatives, those spirits that constituted his blood, his substance, and that tiny island of memory rooting him in this country. Though he had met his obligations to the past and was satisfied that his duty was done, he did not forget that there was still the second part of the ritual: putting incense in the *butsudan*, the family altar, the way he had learned from his parents. And so, unhurriedly, keeping Keiko in his mind all the while, he retraced his steps, strolled past the gardens, distracted himself examining the markers and the names of the deceased, looking, out of habit, for Japanese surnames.

A short while later, he came across a noisy retinue, a crowd transporting a coffin covered in straps, flowers raining down behind it.

Men in embroidered vests appeared, women in black skirts, escorted by musicians in hats who played curious muliza tunes on violin and saxophone. Despite the fact that Nakamatsu hated tribal activities, the showy procession moved him, the haughty faces outlined in the light, seeming to bob to the music in the background. It was a theatrical display, the sobbing girls, the bright outfits, the exhibition of emotions en plein air, making for a grotesquely baroque impression. There was a cartoonish beauty, Nakamatsu thought, to this abominable relay with the dead body, there was no reason for piteousness, pain transformed into colorful play, beer, racket, into a jubilant primitivism that was still rooted in Catholic ritual. After walking with them for a stretch, Katzuo made his way to the little chapel, crossing paths with the twilight visitors, and examined the stylized iron Christ, then he went out the main gate, and got into a car marooned in the little plaza. He took a deep breath, left behind the woodworking huts, the taxi driver turned up the radio and went down Jirón Áncash, making his way behind Mercado La Parada, and drove the car onto Avenida México, while Katzuo, sprawled in his seat, drowsy perhaps, a bit vague, no expression on his face, stared fixedly at the homes emerging on the hills, among the slopes and dirt steps, little corner markets, junk shops. Those new working-class neighborhoods, those sly faces and bulging bellies, occupying streets and plazas with their barbarian notion of progress, mowing everything down, they aroused in him a hideous panic, and all he could do was resign himself to miserable coexistence. This he had always known, and it was useless to interfere, he would not look at or listen to the confusion of precarious huts, and the sheds with their rat trap breath.

For now, the taxi traveled down Balconcillo toward its destination in Santa Catalina, a middle-class development with its wide unfurling avenues, the buildings two or three stories tall with their gardens, the gardens with their trees, and the trees alongside their tulip bushes. Houses lined up one after the other, with their cornices and subtle ledges, the water tank on the roof, big aluminum-frame windows, security gate in front of the entrance, the car in its spot, and reinforced doors. Nakamatsu got off on Avenida San Eugenio, a lot of Japanese families had settled in the area, among them Hideo, the brother who kept the family *butsudan*. When he entered the home, he saw only Sumie, his brother's wife, a tan woman of average height, plump arms and flat eyes, groomed like a little doll, who received him in a burgundy housedress and shined shoes, smiling, elegant, and aloof. She slid exquisitely by like scented foam, such that there were no effusive exchanges, no, barely a greeting, and benign conversation, enough to inquire after his siblings: Hirotoku, Angélica, Tókuzan, and Kiotake. The occasions when he saw them were few, a wedding, a wake, an unavoidable celebration, since Katzuo visited nobody, this was his lot, university professor on a meager state salary. The poor relative, unhappy widower, childless, Katzuo lived in a working-class neighborhood in a house inherited from their parents; he felt embarrassment, shame. Hideo, on the other hand, the oldest brother, husband of Sumie, was a propane distributor with a plant in San Luis and six offices across Lima's districts. Tókuzan, another brother, likewise managed three chicken spots and a snack bar in La Molina. Not to mention Angélica and Kiotake, who had an accounting office in San Borja with many firms among their clientele. The siblings were united by a terrible faith, struggling against everyone else, withstanding crises and setbacks to emerge spirited, and they were proud to call themselves the Nakamatsu clan, with in-laws and nieces and nephews, a tangle of relatives. Despite these opportunities for support, Katzuo was uncompromising with himself, business bored him, and he had always been disposed to austerity, the rigor of ideas and the search for a voice of his own, no weaknesses, no rumbles; that's why, with no illusions, he no longer visited the successful old friends of the family, the Goyas, the Tomitas, and so many other *nisei*.

And so, claiming he was in a rush, Katzuo walked over to the *butsudan*, family altar, in the living room, opened a small package, and placed the *okashis*, the Japanese sweets he'd bought for the occasion, on a plate. He lit the *senko*, the incense, and gave a reverent greeting in front of the spirit tablets, he paid tribute to the ashes of his parents and other dead, even Keiko. Without further ado, diligent in his duties, Katzuo said goodbye to Sumie. About thirty minutes had passed, night had fallen on the streets of Santa Catalina, between the houses with their domestic air, the dimmed lights, and the cold passing over his face, he thought that he had played his cards decorously, in his personal language. In any case, he had gone a step further, taken the initiative, no choice but to deal with his private matters, serenely, unshakeable, hands in his pockets, plumbing the blackness of the gardens, no pedestrians, no witnesses, his glasses falling off his nose. Obstinately perhaps, or resentfully, though without bitterness, Katzuo wondered, why was he different from his siblings, why had he chosen another path, did he have some other animal's smell, other skin, other eyes, other instincts, why was he nobody, why always this lack, the helplessness, the rending, an emptiness: why death?

5

NAKAMATSU HAD ALWAYS conducted himself with discretion and restraint, never making a misstep. And so he didn't have any issues arranging his retirement, and then he lodged an appeal for his readmission to the university. In the meantime, he dusted off his little unfinished story and got to work diligently in the mornings; he felt it was necessary and that he was finally adequately mature for the task. In his tortured and unruly childhood, when voices and specters had twined in his mind, he had heard of Etsuko Untén, a haughty Japanese man, friend of his father. The facts were more or less unreal, or perhaps domestic, and he didn't remember much. But Etsuko Untén, in the face of imminent war, had accepted his fate; proud and harsh, he battled himself, and confronted the country unarmed, impelled by his strict code of honor, and his desire to die. Seeing as how he had considered his dignity beyond blemish, Etsuko Untén, rash or not, fumbling or not, mad or absurd, had been utterly faithful to his brutal style.

Naturally, after writing, in the afternoons he enjoyed walks to the parks, or went on long strolls around La Molina or a seaside spot to the south. His activities followed their course, and his creative energy dissolved into imagination; no matter what happened, he had to expect the inevitable, carrying out his own routines, exactly the same as the day before, no pauses or anguish. Sometimes he visited Masao Uchida, and they talked in a confusion of laughter, drinking wine and smoking; on other occasions, Katzuo crossed Parque El Porvenir in search of the philosophers on extension Lucanas, Mundito Rivera and Don Quinto Vargas or Don Paco Mármol, who discussed their domestic burdens, apparatuses used by suicide victims, and the fights between lowlifes that had the streets by the throat. Likewise, he stocked up on provisions at the little market on Unanue and La Mar, then chatted with Señito Constantina, the butcher, and didn't forget to greet Moscote, a disheveled mestizo who sang chicha songs. He might also visit Palestina, a blind woman in a wheelchair who specialized in consoling lonely men and wayward women with a simple stroke of one's head aura.

All the same, never is the ground level nor the cycles unchanging, and there were sluggish afternoons when Katzuo felt no desire to leave the house, or listen to music, or turn on the TV. To combat those useless hours, he knew perfectly well what to do, occupying himself with what he'd always done since Keiko died: crochet from a bulky skein of yarn. He sat at the desk in the living room, and as so many times before, taken over by the needlework, he began his phlegmatic ritual. With his fingers moving, his task involved working the yarn and the hook, little hexagons in different colors that some faraway day would be forged into a blanket of incalculable size. In reality, the finished product didn't matter, just the method, his feet in their precise position, back glued to his chair, sitting straight, his head bowed, his gaze focused on his hands, not adjusting his torso, nothing on his mind, no images, inhaling and exhaling through his nose. When he achieved full arm, finger, eye, and ear synchronization, and was attuned only to the pulsation of his breath, no needs, no surprises, only then he reached a quiet composure, and murky control of his consciousness. Through the years Katzuo had perfected his movements, and he could crochet even in full darkness, through touch, as everything was reduced to a homogenous process, effortlessly repeated throughout the long moment. And he allowed himself to flow out of his pores, his belly, his blood, his entrails, unspeaking, unseeing, armless, legless, no memories, no thoughts. There was no space, there was no time; following his hazy course, he managed to snuff out the fatigue, the hunger, the nostalgia, up to that unreal moment, when the afternoon was no longer afternoon, and the evening was not evening, and nothing was nothing.

In that instant, just as Katzuo had found tranquility, he began hearing birdsong coming from the bedroom. At first he ignored it, as it was an indistinct noise, and continued his labors without faltering, but the birds' clamoring grew loud, a concert of chirps and trills emerging bountiful from a recessed grove, with its greenery, flowers, shrubs, and open country. Intrigued, Nakamatsu paused his activity and got up to see what was happening in his bedroom. He turned on the lights and found nothing except the wardrobe, his bed, and the folding screen, and all the same the happening was still there in the air, immaterial and real, expanding onto the ceiling, like a rain chorus, or a mild waterfall. He didn't say a word, untroubled, he looked up at a spot in the air, focused his mind on that invisible stretch, and then he heard, even more intensely, the keening of the birds; beating wings, a rustle of leaves, babbling spills of water, and the breath of a creek, as if all of that were leaving, in his mouth, a sediment of thickets, overgrown scrub, and untamable nature. He stood there captivated, Katzuo did, he couldn't believe it, it seemed impossible, where was it coming from, the buzzing, the sensorial trills, the unceasing clicking, the colorful wild birds, he was surrounded by it all, absorbed it all, as he would've images of brooks, gullies, precipices. It might have been a brief second, five minutes perhaps; in reality, Nakamatsu, surprised, withdrawn into himself, couldn't pinpoint exactly how long the happening lasted, the miracle occurred again and again over the next two weeks, intermittently, whether in the morning, in the afternoon, or at any hour of the night, and every time he was left astonished by that sensation of an unusual beauty.

Out of curiosity, Katzuo inquired with his apartment neighbors to the left and right whether someone was keeping an aviary or hearing choruses of birds, larks, or canaries. And the answers in the negative were unanimous, not Señor García, nor Señora Palomino, nor Guillermo from Piura, nobody, had animals in their homes, and they hadn't heard anything, and there was no way the chirping could have filtered through the adjoining walls. Katzuo didn't make a commotion, he understood that the happening was a result of chance, a fault in the ceiling, a joke or irregularity, in any case, like he was in a bubble; he walked around in his living room, the bedroom, grinding his teeth, hands behind his back, in the kitchen, the taste of virgin earth in his mouth and feral scents on the brain. What at first had been ecstasy and astonishment gradually turned into uncertainty, maybe his mind was playing tricks on him, maybe he was going insane, wasn't reality itself often incoherent and even absurd? Nakamatsu smoked, mild-mannered and uncertain perhaps, continued to move around, drink coffee, grind his teeth, untrusting, he even went out to walk down 28 de Julio, about fifteen blocks, to take shelter in Campo de Marte, where

43

he proceeded to pace past the fences, the gardens, the different paths and fountains, but it was as if he hadn't left his bedroom, he couldn't see anything, not the tipas, the cypresses, the molles. A sensation in bursts of uselessness and neglect, slow rotations in his narrow circle, until the unplanned moment when he found himself in front of the park's elegant Japanese bridge, that structure made of cement, wood, and granulated stone. He saw it against the blue of the sky, and his eyes clouded over, he shed tears, inhaling the air's fragrance; he sighed, throbbing, heard the sounds of the cars on the avenue, and once again, inexorable, as on so many other occasions, he felt the death drive in his intestines. A sudden explosion, a discharge of emotion, muddled blinking, the wobbling old body, legs disjointed, despondent before the abyss and the utter darkness. He had to sit down on a bench, Katzuo seemed to shrink, he felt ashamed, those strolls, his very life, the books he had loved, everything settled into emptiness, like it had never existed, like there was no justification, for him, for his body, for his dreams, for anything at all.

It's very likely he roamed through the streets, unembarrassed, unfeeling, through mazes of houses, dense copses of trees, working-class developments, and traffic. When he resurfaced into consciousness, he found himself in his house, sitting at the desk chair, gazing at the bookcase, dissolved and wilted, hands in his lap, not moving his legs, not a single muscle, inhaling and exhaling, not thinking, not feeling, completely static, rocklike, eyes locked on the air. He was able to spend many unscathed hours in that forced watchfulness, sleepless, tireless, ominously helpless. Naturally, forged like iron in adversity, perhaps morose, Nakamtasu withstood desperation's battering over several days, staying in his house, scarcely disrupted by visits from Mundito Rivera or Don Paco Mármol, the street corner philosophers from the bench on Lucanas, who brought him up to date on what was happening in the neighborhood. Armored inside himself, the patient Katzuo revisited anecdotes from his childhood, a string of voices unraveled into his consciousness, then braced the Star pistol against his temple, exactly the way he had wanted, remembering, doubting, step by step, until one clear Tuesday night with a full moon, when the stars were auspicious. He had to visit, and eventually say goodbye to, Juancito Miyazaki, a friend from his youth and the only *nisei* who was a learned, competent reader of the Bible and decipherer of enigmas, who with his indomitable acuity was capable of understanding any and all jagged states of the spirit, of dampening sorcery and dispelling hesitations. In the middle of 28 de Julio, Katzuo looked up and was enraptured by the reflections of the moon, thinking about the charms of the night and the blackness of the world.

And how could you not, oh ludicrous Katzuo, starry-eyed with life, mechanical and inscrutable, get into a taxi and arrive ten minutes later at Plaza Ruiz Gallo in Lince, at the ramshackle Midori, the little restaurant stuffed with tables and chairs, the smell of sawdust, customers eating, and there was your friend Juan Miyazaki at the register. There was nothing to it, Katzuo, he received you with open arms, overflowing joy, and the two of you sat down at a table to the side, without witnesses, drank a glass of rum, aged rum, and looked at each other in silence, each seeking the other's eyes. There was mutual understanding. Breathing slowed. You understood each other. And so with no preamble, no snags, as if smoking a cigarette, from the bottom of your heart, Katzuo, unsure whether or not he could hear you, you issued a stream of invectives, admonishments, violent phrases, raging circumlocutions, a river loaded with noise, animal panting, stutters mixed with guffaws, tirades, then the chirping of birds, geysers, flowing rain, waterfalls, greenery, confusion of countenances, Japanese laborers on haciendas, the arrogant Etsuko Untén, Avenida Salaverry, Parque de la Exposición, and its depraved sakura bringing death. As he gave his hallucinatory account, the tormented Katzuo managed to say: "They're chasing me." And Juan Miyazaki asked: "Who's chasing you?" And Katzuo Nakamatsu answered: "I have ghosts inside my head." The two of them had been examining each other in silence, face to face, the table in between, motionless in their chairs, countenances frozen, maintaining eye contact, no need to breathe, old comrades, for ten, for fifteen, for thirty unbreakable minutes, no rhyme or reason, when Juancito Miyazaki got up from his seat, disappeared, returned shortly thereafter with a sheaf of cards in his hand, shuffling, extracting. And here, my friends, Katzuo Nakamatsu chose four cards at random, of his own free will, and laid them on the table. And Juan Miyazaki looked at the cards, saturated with silence, a long time he was paused looking at them, and seeing the cups, the aces, and the queens, he had no recourse but to exclaim: "Shit! You're going insane!" And Katzuo Nakamatsu repeated: "Insane?" And Juan Miyazaki confirmed: "Insanity and death side by side!"

6

IN THOSE DAYS, Nakamatsu had an obsessive recurring dream. He would be visiting the streets of San Borja on a sunny afternoon, and there he would see a beautiful tiled roof on one of the big old houses, boughs twining in a small grove, and gardens, and rose bushes. Crossing, on López de Ayala, a park full of cassowaries, he noted cornices, plated partition walls, and traveled down glinting avenues. When he arrived at Boulevard, he would start to feel as though he were being stalked, obscenely spied upon, shadows moving behind his back; he heard cloaked laughter, suspicious voices, degrading insults. Curiously, when he turned around, nobody was there, not even a hint of another person; all the same, the sky was blanketed in violet, and he began to feel suffocated. He'd ramble aimlessly through parks, the houses having drawn drearily back into themselves, the streets shut off, closed over like tunnels, and he realized he was wandering in concentric circles, as if walking along a spiderweb, more and more stifled, without escape, gone mad, overcome. In that moment, Katzuo would wake up, returning to reality drenched in sweat, eyes in torment, oppressed by the voices and images from his sleep.

Those gory nights repeated inextinguishable, and they did nothing but accentuate that deep conviction of his, since the things that remained undetermined, who was following him, were closer than ever. And so he walked around the living room, arms behind his back, past the bedroom, and the only thing he regretted was having reached the final bend, old and eroded, clinging to a routine lacking in foresight, unable to leave his body, his personal prison, that hideaway consisting of equal parts importance, sufferings, and joys. Any initiative he might take would not alter his irrevocable course, and in that instant he made a decision for his personal gratification, to visit the antique stores in Barranco. He bought a gray felt hat, one of those that had been stylish in the forties, as well as a dark canvas coat that fell below the knees. He also purchased a pair of vintage tortoiseshell glasses, and picked out a blue tie with white pinstripes, and spruced up some narrow-legged trousers, and selected a wooden cane with a reinforced handle. Because this is how it was: by that time in his rituals of farewell, he had discerned that he was to transform himself and dress like Etsuko Untén, that unbridled friend of his father's, to look the way

Untén looked in the photos he kept in his files. And at the same time, this was a means of expressing his recognition of the beloved Martín Adán, and becoming exactly like him, taking on the same reactions, the same gestures, the same gait, the same spirit of estrangement.

Dressed in this way, he turned out on the dusty streets of La Mar and Bausate y Meza, going to the little market in search of provisions, or conversing with the street-corner philosophers on the bench on Lucanas, or eating lunch at Juanita Terukina's restaurant. Nothing mattered anymore, it was like time had become circular, and he could resurrect the past untroubled. He went around on microbuses, attended recitals, bought coffee at little stands, took his solitary strolls up parks and down boulevards, always with his outmoded hat on, the antiquated glasses, his brooding whiskers, the unflappable relic of a coat, and the cane made of guayacán. And he incited curiosity every time, facing insults and abuse from foolish people, but they were of no interest to Nakamatsu; he was unaffected, did not react, his walk inflexible, looking at the sky absorbed, focusing inward, withdrawn and aloof, lost in meditation. Of the former professor Katzuo Nakamatsu, always irreproachable, polite, only vestiges remained; he seemed more elusive, wary, and distant, unresponsive to greetings or jokes, clinging to the old ways. Among the neighbors on Bausate y Meza grew the legend of the misunderstood Nakamatsu: mad, hallucinating, with his antediluvian air, and his delirious habits, like the upsetting howls that came from his apartment in the pre-dawn hours. When all was said and done, nobody knew who Etsuko Untén was, that anonymous Japanese man who, when war dawned on Lima, took up his own battle in defense of what he considered his country's honor. Katzuo loved the stormy aspects of Etsuko Untén, the punishing existence of his final years as he sacrificed everything yet remained tenacious and unchanging in his passion, left unchipped by the affronts. Now in old age, struggling against the tide, at the margins of silence, Nakamatsu could unabashedly render his admiration, and reproduce, in his consciousness, the private pulse of Etsuko Untén, which was none other than the feeling of Martín Adán, both uprooted, forgotten in a corner, and reviled.

At the very least, Katzuo's notes and diaries from this time abound in observations about his reality, and his longing, within that deeply desired inferno, to retreat into himself. After all, from childhood Nakamatsu had understood pain and suffering to be vehicles of purification, paths toward perfection; he would have liked, without faintness or weakness, to lacerate his own flesh, as a way of erasing his unwholesome I. Faced with life's mundanity, his most personal beliefs were, outwardly, an absolute coldness, dissociation from all things, austerity in pleasure, and frugality of the flesh. For years, in his youth before the death of Keiko, he'd been, like any other man, clumsy, sloppy, a little criollo improviser: he had friends, visited cantinas, loved fun, was a restless gambler. Bitter experience, crises and dangerous situations, had made him return to what he considered his natural Asiatic roots, but with no friends, or people to shelter him, just as he did now, he could turn back only to confront darkness itself, following instinct, turning toward his own nullity, taciturn and fierce. And now this is the critical moment when he alters his attire and moves his very life toward Etsuko Untén / Martín Adán, to confront the contempt in his environs, since he's already regarded as a paranoiac with his outdated getup and shapeless madness, but all of that leaves him indifferent, aloof, owing no explanation to anyone, as if his heart weren't human. There, with his gray hat, sorry raincoat, and uncompromising cane, he strolled the streets on his afternoon walks, even, curiously, at the height of summer, paying no mind to the heat or embarrassment, to the barking dogs, or to the drug addicts and chicha lovers on the corners begging for money. It was under these circumstances, while searching along Avenida Cuba for one of the big houses with a Republic-era patio, that he inadvertently found himself lost in a bend, under the shade of a magnificent grove of ceibos growing beside the road, their shining branches laden with flowers. With this unexpected discovery, Katzuo felt a terrible spasm in his intestines; in the afternoon's yellowed scenery, the crowns of the ceibos flexed against the sky, their fragrance ignited and their green shoots gaudy, unconquered. He looked at them in that endless instant, and immediately heard a sob, babbling, and then peculiar voices welling up from the ground and the roots of the trees, like groans rising in the distance, scarcely audible on that springlike afternoon. Those voices sounded like a brood of flies, and in a monologue they intoned, "You are at your origins. Do not forget them, that group of Japanese men, all under twenty-three years of age, who reached the coast of Peru in 1918 on the cargo ship Anyo Maru, prideful and phosphorescent, who for better and for worse disembarked from a wide barge at an inlet in Cerro Azul, contracted as labor for the Hacienda Santa Bárbara." Standing in front of the ceibos and their fragile beauty, Katzuo listened to the chorus of voices and it was like he had always been waiting for them, feeling no remorse, unfurrowing his brow, master of himself, level and immutable, because these were the ghosts and legends that had swarmed his childhood, those phrases arising in dreams, running through his head, sliding through his blood, diluting themselves into his panting breaths.

"There they were, your father Zentaró and the clever Etsuko Untén, dressed in coarse Western clothes, canvas jackets, white pants, and glossy shoes, hats tight on their heads. Poor provincials from Okinawa, they passed through the town of Cañete on a cart driven by a black foreman, amid the insults, jeers, rocks, and ridicule of the mestizos, cholos, and heavy toothless women, who would not allow these foreign undesirables, contracted to do manual labor, to take away their jobs and their children's daily bread. Not in Cañete, not on the haciendas, not in Lunahuaná, not in Mala, not in Lurín, not in the surrounding towns: the Japanese weren't wanted anywhere, don't forget that, never forget, nobody was waiting for us, nobody opened their arms, they detested us rancorously, hostilely, hatefully. That was how we arrived in this country."

For days afterward, for weeks even, Nakamatsu wandered the streets around Bausate y Meza and Parque El Porvenir in bewilderment, a wraithlike being, cheeks pale, lips pursed, chin tipped down, showing off his useless hat, his unsteady cane, his vintage jacket. There they all were, the chipped street corners, the scrap merchants swarming with their tricycle carts, and that spill of working-class faces, small windows, power lines, and rag merchants with their junk, while he, Katzuo, walked, solemn, swaying absurdly in the heat, exactly as if in a reverie, pondering these voices from the past. That sobbing, mumbling, growling reminded him of his turbid childhood, when his head had been full of those wraithlike old Japanese, and even with his eyes open, completely awake, Katzuo saw, in the barges at port, in the hills, behind the gullies, in the hard earth of the cotton plantations, feverish Japanese laborers bustling on the patios of their quarters among chickens and guinea pigs. It wasn't him, it was a whirlwind of corrupted voices, chimerical scenes, unreal images that came and went, carving swirls and squalls into the imagination and the heart, whether in the mornings as he wrote his novel about the unfathomable Etsuko

Untén, or during his afternoon strolls on some street in San Luis, or perhaps at the internet cafés where he listened to zarzuelas. And all the while, Katzuo asked himself in his anguish: Who were they? Did they perhaps come from one of death's zones? Why had they burst into his head as winding stories and murmurs? He truly could not explain it, and paced from the living room to the bedroom, through the kitchen, sighing by the air shaft, talking to himself, grinding his teeth, hands behind his back, smoking incessantly, glimpsing the confusion his life had turned into. Was he a madman? Was he raving? Who was he? Maybe a dark and deadly being had taken over his body? And as his brain spun with immense celestial questions, for measureless days he forgot to eat, shave, bathe. Nevertheless, when his confusion lifted and he had days at peace, and he went out for his afternoon strolls, one of those nights when he found himself at his desk, looking at the shelves of books, absorbed in the flow of his consciousness, nothing on his mind, feeling nothing, in the depths of emptiness, once again his musical birds came back: those trills, that picturesque chirping filling his bedroom with a taste of cliffs, the babbling creek, the scent of oregano and lúcuma fruit fumes, the grasses of the meadow. And like always, Katzuo gazed rapturously in the air, and continued to be astonished, with an astonishment that was almost bliss, since this was a snippet of nature in all its splendor. The peculiar thing this time was that amid the foliage were the voices of his forebears, that chorus of faraway words, those cries that earlier had emerged from the blooming ceibos: "For the Japanese there was no mercy; on the contrary, the foremen and their underlings sent them to tear down the mountain because it was a task not even a black man would accept. Sapped by the sun, they were forced to work the sterile earth, the shrubbed expanses, rocky debris, rubble, darnel, and excoriations of the terrain they were meant to level, and contend with swamps, there too making piles of brush, bracken, tree trunks, and pests. And the cholos and their Indian wives, the Indian sharecroppers, the shepherds, the foundry workers, and the drivers crowded on the promontories to see the spectacle of those hideous Japanese, your father Zentaró and Etsuko Untén among them, with their hoes and pickaxes, naked in the heat, entering the rugged scrub to clear land not our own, that they slashed with fire, that they chiseled tooth and nail, and suffered through in every worted field, exhausting themselves, swallowing lizards, just so those mestizos circled on the promontory with their children and wives could exclaim: Oh, those beastly Japanese, they're just like animals."

Enthralled, Katzuo listened infinitely to those rippling burbles, the testimony of a past sealed off, in the quiet of his bedroom, face set, lips pursed, teeth creaking, as the bodiless voices wisped into the air, as in his childhood, when his head had been saturated with specters, those beings forgotten in a distant corner, making labyrinthine rounds through his consciousness. Unable to do anything, they hovered ravenously, swirling, their cloistered smells, their swollen greenery: "And for thirty-six months they suffered extortions and indignities, before the two young men escaped from the hacienda. Don't forget, they were poor foreigners, with no hope for shelter, roaming alone across the terraces, far from the towns where the police could catch them. And only at the end did Etsuko Untén and your father Zentaró leave, but they didn't flee to Lima, where the people were unruly and malevolent, but rather to the tambos around Cañete, hiding like maroons. They bought supplies and two mules to make a wood cart, with a Japanese flag on it in spite of everything. They went to the workers' quarters on ranches, visited lost villages and boarding houses full of laborers, the isolated fields of Indian sharecroppers, clambering up foothills, avoiding the bridle paths, to sell fruit, jerked meat, spirits and chicha, cotton fabric, lard, and salt, and were even accompanied by their goats and errant chickens. They were unrestrained and crazy, and at night, the two of them, drunk and furious, singing in Uchinago, the language of Okinawa, cheered each other up, beating their chests, slapping their thighs, and they challenged the hamlet dwellers, any of those crude chutos or mestizos who wanted to face them, to bare-knuckled beatdowns for a fistful of coins. Hardened by those bouts, unwilling to suffer defeat, your father Zentaró and Etsuko Untén, they never yielded, because these were duels between men, vindications of honor, suspended above violent clouds of dust, bodies naked, blows bloody, mercilessly pummeled until they fell, senseless, arrogant. They led these savage lives to prove to themselves that they were unstoppable, because they upheld the mark of their race, and were compelled to be relentless, hard, even in a foreign land, resolving their internal humiliation and confusion with fists. They didn't want to be trampled, that's why they slept on the ground, wrapped in Indian pelts, their shirts itchy with sweat, enduring the cruel cold and the intransigent sun, and spent a handful of years in the elements, making money. Never forget, those are your origins, seeds of the pain, those roving, unfaltering men, no day, no night, no cries, no fatigue, not a single complaint, only endless punishment, always a stony jut to the lips, like nothing mattered."

7

IT'S POSSIBLE Nakamatsu was now entering his most critical stage. The situation is thus. Katzuo would walk in the Parque de la Reserva among the shrubs and the sage, coalescing with the green and the stone steps, observing the water spilling from the jets and the twining bougainvillea. Above the fresh scents, the weather is pleasant, he passes under arches and colonnades, and in the back, the blue drop of the sky. Nothing foretells anything, it might have even been a humdrum afternoon, but all the same, they barge in, his torrent of birds, the chorus of bodiless voices, and that familiar history flowing ruthlessly, labyrinthine, lambasting his head, his mind, in an effusion of legends and forgotten histories. Nakamatsu focuses on the air, absorbed, watches it all move past, set against the atmosphere, and his body goes rigid, motionless, face reserved, gaze lost to the clouds, eyes glassy, as if contemplating the emptiness. He looked to be hallucinating, and despite his coldness and stony attitude, from the depths of his being Katzuo was wondering, why this abrupt vortex, that torment twirling and whirling in his consciousness, like a fit of noise, a rale, phonations, and emissions incarnating ghosts and spirits, forgotten and now nonexistent, which he himself could not quite understand. In any case, stuporous and dispassionate, he was left dazed by those visions, no choice but doubt, pondering, peeling apart, rethinking, and probing amid tears: why the murmuring, that faraway sobbing, the moans. And in that instant, as he continued his stroll, he sensed, like a hex behind his back, hissing and insults, obscene hollering, brazen shades dragging past, beseeching him by name, embedded. Nevertheless, Katzuo did not move his head, nor turn his neck, nor twist his body around, because there was no one there, he knew he was alone, terribly alone. They were unspeakable, indistinct shadows, strange beings that hounded him from death's borders, there they were, after him, diabolical, bamboozling him with their purring, their laughter, sardonic when it wasn't bellowing and antagonizing, flattening him with their suffocating murmurs, with their profanities, snuffling and hawking up phlegm.

Katzuo Nakamatsu looked afflicted, with no answer for his urges, and for inexorable nights and days, he seemed to lose heart, invaded by an urge toward death, as if there was nothing but confusion, wisps of haze, in his mind, nothing to yearn for but picking up the Star and pulling the trigger, or maybe banging his head against the wall, and shouting and howling like an animal caged within the four walls of his home. It was under those circumstances that, to give channel to his animal desire for extinction, he picked up his strange habit of walking in the depths of the night, at two or three in the morning, arrayed always in his relic of a hat, the irreversible coat, his ancient shoes, grasping the unbending cane. He made his sleepless way down 28 de Julio, Brasil, or Paseo Colón, looking up at the sky, absorbed, auscultating the silence of the stars, in an apparent state of calm or contempt for the world, sitting on benches in the street, parking himself in shadowy corners, confronting chicha lovers and lowlifes, entering the bar Campari on Pasaje María Auxiliadora, it's possible he was attempting to explain to himself the secret of his meaningless, rootless, aimless life. Objectively, the surroundings are something like this: the half-lit bar, a wall at the back, the glass-topped counter, chairs crammed in, a smattering of patrons. At one of the tables next to the window, señor Nakamatsu and his hat, his whiskers, and his cane, sitting with a cup of weak coffee, silent, unmoving, preoccupied, the same posture: eyes staring into the emptiness, focusing on the air, not hearing, not feeling, not speaking. He is like an impassive shadow, completely static, no glimmer of life, not an inkling, unamazed, like nothing matters, not him, not anyone. And the minutes pass, half hours, whole hours, and there he remains dauntless, lips fixed, cheeks tight in that contemptuous grimace, uncompromising, featureless. And the following night, at two or three in the morning, once again he will repeat his movements down 28 de Julio, crossing the same unchanging streets, the same feelings descending when he reaches Avenida Brasil, with the same gray coat, the same shoes, his same impenetrable cane, to sit in front of the same window at Campari, drink his weak coffee, envisage the same images, in the same half-light, to think about the same things, if one could call it thinking.

And perhaps when he grew bothered or weary, he would, with the same indifference, sink down another rung in his obstinacy, venturing down Avenida Grau with its circus tent in the dark night, on that street with its porn theaters, flophouses, prostitutes, crackling smokers, bums in the open elements, and urchins trading sex for a plate of food. And he would continue on his way, his intractable lot, like Etsuko Untén / Martín Adán had done in the days of yore, on so many indecent nights, looking for seedy establishments, vile dives, armored in his dignity, in his unfaltering hat, in his crosshatched tie. And it never bothered Katzuo to enter the irreal Farolito, a miserable den, where he would run into shady teenagers, their colorful jackets and their impossible heads of hair, and take immense pleasure from their lean faces, ravenous eyes, and the gleam of their olive skin. He was attracted to their strong scents, he examined the join of their red lips, the haptic movement of their necks, those angular hands. And looking, tasting, burning with desire, and craving their fantasy bodies, with their rough-hewn scents, their perennial vices, the choked yelling, and the coming and going and the churning of feet. He knew, this was his own personal hell, pleading for a caress, for an obscure kiss, Nakamatsu continued sitting in the same position, static, unmoving, secretly watching, covert, hat on his head, archaic glasses, weathering contempt, shamefaced, tenacious, impassive as he waited. And night after night, he would go back there, dissolute, his eyes adjusting to the tangle and the rabble, his seedy surroundings in the Farolito bar, sprawled in his seat, in any old corner, inhaling perhaps, directing, sublimating, perched near his weak coffee, the explosion of joy, the private flavor of the abyss, in the prolongation of his helplessness, sitting there with the same absent face, the same elbows on the table, the same exhausted expression, the same abstract eyes, nothing to feel, nothing to say, nothing to weep over. Withdrawn, possibly, apart from him, above Katzuo's head, expiration's hatch had opened, he had been left to his own malign nature, his attraction to perversion, and perhaps he grasped it when the insolent men asked for change, or when he was engrossed in conversation with the unerring prostitutes, or when the sickly teenagers appeared, and they closed around him with their bald insinuations: he touched the world with his hand, untortured and unembarrassed, his flesh cleaved open, he soaked in opaque pleasures, miserable joy, and clots of contentment.

~

In that period, Katzuo broke past his boundaries without letting anything upset him, as if trying to humble himself, drained by his longing to be tortured. He slept little and poorly, complained of horrible aches, the body's uselessness, and his inexorable old age. He was still writing his novel about Etsuko Untén, and the Japanese men who accompanied him in his struggle, unbending, in a territory and country that was utterly adverse. In the afternoons, his companion was me, Benito Gutti, his colleague of many years at the university, and the author of this report. We were not friends, nevertheless, after he was dismissed from his teaching duties, I don't know why he came to me, stammering, his gaze spent, and between polite circumlocutions, vaguely insinuated that there was no meaning left, his life had already been nothing but a confused labyrinthine roundabout before the fog rolled in. I was surprised by his words, his impassive resolve, and above all by his defenseless air, he seemed helpless, consumed by his fixation on death, his eyes evasive behind his thick glasses. And so I began visiting him at his house on La Mar, we ate lunch together, taking long strolls down avenues and through parks, conversing about Martín Adán, the scandalous poet he so admired, whom Katzuo imitated and wanted deeply to reproduce, in his sentiments, dissolution, absurdity. Despite his unsociable, impenetrable character, Nakamatsu possessed an admirable spiritual rectitude, and a fierce defensive instinct that prevented him from talking about himself, as if he were seeking refuge behind a carapace, unwilling to effect any gestures, opinions, impulses, or hopes. He expressed himself in monosyllables, measuring his words, mistrustful, as if we were all his enemies, and for no discernible reason he would go quiet, looking up at the sky, shy, confounding.

By then, whenever he heard those unfaltering voices in his head, and when he felt pursued by dark shadows, in his share of the good and the bad, in his trance, Nakamatsu was more inclined toward the morbid interest that drove him to dark passion, uninterested in the respectable life, or academic prestige, or codes of reason. Now, quaking, he would go meet the lethargic tarts in Parque Manco Cápac, sit sensuous until dawn with the misunderstood young fellows on Avenida Garcilaso de la Vega, and in the nightclubs on Rufino Torrico he bawled with the displaced hookers, the third-rate pimps, and the veteran homosexuals. This is the scene, more or less: the interior of the Las Magnolias brothel on Avenida Colonial; a short counter with seats and bottles, raucous music, mirrored walls, a dance floor, then the hookers' cubbies. The multicolor lights spinning, lavender and cinnamon perfume, jesters doing the rounds, and nevertheless, sitting on a chair, Katzuo comes into view, focused on his weak coffee, looking at nobody, not hearing the commotion, eyes staring at the air, abstract, not moving, muscles taut, his breath lethargic, cheeks raspy, lips sealed, with his hat, coat, and the archaic spectacles, perfectly absent. In any case, he was attracted to the sweat, the heat of the decrepit night, the panting dance floor, the drowsy lights, the booming noise, the motley smells, like there was no limit to any of it, nor pleasure even, not the naked bodies, everything there whirling, impervious, in the milky unwholesome air.

Nakamatsu had the appearance of an inert spirit. He was like a clump, everything converged in him. And whether he wanted or not, this bestowed upon him a blameless elation, free of plaintive questions. And when he felt most acutely that life was degrading, all of a sudden, without his prompting, in the depths of his body, the chirping of his birds would resurge, the chorus of wild fowl, the forest scents bursting, the exuberant plashing of the creek: all of it filling him, all of it transfiguring him. In any circumstance, at any moment, on the street, at home, in any one of the dens or bordellos, they would return once again, lavishly, abundantly. And against that backdrop, gleaming foliage and curling scrub, those voices of his emerged, like they always did, from his past, the sobs, that keening, like they were crossing hills, like they were coming from another world, their schizophrenic murmurs arrived, to chant that Etusko Untén, that arrogant strapping young man, had retreated to a town on the northern coast, and not just that, always the clever charmer, he had gotten hold of ten hectares, on a bet and a pledge of marriage. Then he settled down, planted cotton, and with that same rage and avarice he even got married before the church to a Peruvian woman, the daughter of a rural teacher, his protector, but they never consummated the marriage, because for Etsuko Untén, jumbling the races was impossible, especially because he was Japanese. Proud and impassive, but above all stingy, more solitary than ever, he abhorred the town, the people, and the land that had seen him grow from a man without a cent in his pocket into a modest businessman, and dissatisfied, out of depravation, calculatedness, bitterness, he established a brothel where he himself, along with his wife, oversaw the wayward women. Never forget, in the vicissitudes of life, the decisions are complex, morality is always ambiguous, and so Etsuko Untén upheld his dignity, above the antipathy, condemnation, and rumors, committed to the business, leasing land for other Japanese people to farm, and it was only when he heard that war was imminent that he repudiated his marriage, liquidated his brothel and all of its concoctions, and for patriotic reasons relocated to Lima in 1941, to join the struggle for Japan and its heroic expansion. Etsuko Untén knew *Nihon* could not be defeated, and that's why he sought out your father Zentaró and other fellow countrymen to get organized, and in this enemy country where everyone loathed us, he came back to organize a group of patriots and fight for victory, it didn't matter that we were being held captive, with no weapons, militias, or resources. But in reality, your father Zentáro was no longer the same man, he had retreated, he had children and a bodega in Barrios Altos, and all their fellow countrymen turned their backs on him. Etsuko Untén had faith in his imperial majesty's army, they wouldn't abandon us in foreign territory, where we were trapped and despised, we were not the ones who unleashed the war, he said at the top of his lungs, dressed scrupulously, like a gentleman, he who had been a crude raggedy troublemaker, now sporting a bowtie, impeccable black jacket, superb vest, smart trousers with high socks, and black calfskin shoes. It was important to maintain self-esteem, *Nihon* was above pity, even when the government confiscated property owned by Japanese people, and they pursued and ridiculed us, we were never going to surrender, even when they circulated lists of names to deport us and ours to internment camps in Texas. He visited this and that place, established halls and clubs, exhorting us to close ranks in those tearful years, creating pockets of resistance, listening day and night to NHK for news, waiting for the proclamation of the imperial army's victory, because we were invincible, and we had never lost a single war. That was Etsuko Untén, never forget him, and to top off his arrogance, he flaunted himself on the boulevard on Grau, because he had to show himself, not defeated, capitulating, or beggared, but rather the race's irrepressible pride embodied, with his hat, the dogged cane, bowtie, and provocateur's manners. On that boulevard of Yankee war policy, he walked slumberously by, eyes keen, with that measured placid gait, totally other, high and mighty, then he entered the bars full of irredeemable cholos and whites. Amid the vapors, the murmurs, the tobacco smoke and the alcohol, between hatred and rancor, he flagged down a glass of cascarilla, and with gloved hands, refined gestures, hat on his head, holding his breath, peering sidelong, keeping his distance, exclusive and untouchable, after twenty minutes, suddenly, solitary, unsociable, unruly, he slammed his hand down on the table in a resounding blow as if he wanted everyone to hear, and slowly drank his glass of cascarilla, brazen, impudent, and then unhurriedly, like he had all the time in the world, he left a couple coins on the table and walked away from all the astonished faces, whistling "Kimigayo," the Japanese national anthem, so that everyone would understand that *Nihon* was victorious, nobody could defeat us, even when we were living in an enemy country.

8

A ND NOW, WRAPPED in the secret of death and alienation, Katzuo
Nakamatsu, purified by instinct, strolled one afternoon around
Plaza Carrión across from Hospital Dos de Mayo. Facing the aged
fig trees, sitting on one of the benches, as on so many other occasions, he saw the inviolable Martin Adán move past, dressed exactly
like he was, with the same gestures, the same guts, the same halting
restraint. They recognized each other in the rabid afternoon sun,
smiled simultaneously, examining each other, like vagrants, snuffling
around each other, giving one another kisses on the cheek, two old
men tender in their domestic caresses, like they had lived together
always. Lack of foresight didn't matter, nothing did; the past, the
future, existence itself could not compare to this illogical moment,
in which Katzuo felt of a piece with Martín Adán, despite the dark

shadows pursuing him, the swirl of voices from his familial past. The irremediable poet fawned over him, and, inseparable, they embarked on the path of ridicule, a path not even Nakamatsu understood, in search of suffering or pleasure, in the dens, near the shacks, the filthy nightclubs, the rundown brothels. And spending time now especially behind Mercado La Parada, on the slopes of Cerro San Cosme, by the flea markets on Nicolás Ayllón, the Yerbateros bus terminal, the intricate walkways of uneven El Agustino. A descent into himself, the inferno he had desired, intimately coveted, because it reflected his mental state: dark unsettled streets, poor neighborhoods, tricksters, junk merchants, welding shops, open lots, cardboard collectors, old clothes, and sly peddlers, razed land and litter. Unshrinking, agitated in the dusty breeze, beyond the fact of his emotional imbalance, perhaps Katzuo was looking for the murderous dagger or bullet at the end of the night, at one of the chicherías, or fields full of festivities, with their perverse homosexuals, or in those cantinas and fly-filled lairs, the hair salons, the bodegas in the hills, where he could spend endless idle hours, focusing on the air, abstract in the emptiness, unaware of whether it was day or night, cold or hot, in a depraved circular timeline. And all the while, despite the insults, the humiliations, and the muggings, even after he lost the hat and the cane, lunatically, inexpressive, he maintained that immutable coldness always, the distance, the mental isolation, as if it were trivial, as if nothing interested him, apathetic, even when his gait became weary, his eyes listless and red, his cheeks sunken, clothes greasy, shoes scruffy, smelling like an old goat.

And thus, with that Asiatic temperament, Katzuo, ghostly perhaps, meandered through nooks and crannies, refuges, hideaways, surly and punctual, with his thick-lensed glasses, with no questions, no hint of quickness, he moved past the stairs up El Pino Hill, between shanties and bald matting, climbing upslope, even as gangs of children sent him tumbling to the ground, and tried to yank his pants down. Nakamatsu didn't defend himself, he scarcely looked up, they spooked and tussled with him, insulting him, shouting, calling out, whacking him; then he would straighten out his clothes, brush off the dust, furiously throw stones, shed tears, martyrized, irritated, and presumably exhausted. On other occasions, he sought out vacant parcels of land, half-built properties, or any secluded hillside, to mix in with the lost addicts, the drunks, the schizophrenics, and the abandoned suicide seekers, prostitutes and queers drinking rat poison. Sitting in the breeze, leaning on the bricks, Katzuo watched them and soaked it all in, listening to their mad guffawing, their absurd stories, back and forth, no rhyme or reason, absolutely vigilant, sorrowful, to such an extent that he became shadowlike, static, unblinking, unmoving, no gleam in his eyes, a senseless stone, no pulse in his mouth, stupefied, retreated into himself, lost in a dark point in space. Then Etsuko Untén arrived, melancholy, his screwdriven gaze, bloodless, quietly wearing clothes similar to Katzuo's, feeble foreigner, ragged and old, pursing his lips, hawking up phlegm, babbling, insisting that it would come, the illusory ship sent by his imperial majesty to gather up all the Japanese in Peru, his only hope in death.

In short, I was worried about Nakamatsu's absence, as he wasn't returning to his house. After asking around, I went looking for him by the lost blocks of Avenida 28 de Julio, in the Manzanillo development, on Avenida Riva Agüero, by the hills of El Agustino, and the slaughterhouse by Yerbateros bus terminal. In his mental map, this was the zone of his most intimate contradictions. I was not surprised to find him completely unkempt, decrepit, as if debased, dusty, absorbed in the sky, looking at the shrews on the corners, there, in the dark cross streets, his shoes cracked, beard wild, skin punished by the sun, his gaze aloof, absent, inhabiting some other reality. I asked him whether this was where he planned to stand face to face with death. And as if he were returning from a desert, he looked up, surprised, making small gestures, hiding his hands, his feet, because he didn't want to be seen like this, alone and abandoned to his fate. And between embarrassment, whispers, and wheezing, from the haze of his consciousness, he began speaking about seeing people's parsimony, the overcrowding, the wretchedness. He spoke of Father Chacho and his acolytes, all of them flying high in the blue sky, crossing slopes, caring for kindergartens, seeding adobe walls in the hills, he had also sung along with rock bands in concert swells, remembered the water truck drivers, discovered crosses stuck into avenues, and people's devotion to Chacalón, and the innumerable cafeterias, and God's admonishments. He saw Sarita Colonia, the people's saint, emerge from dust clouds, sprinkling miracles here and there, healing paraplegics. There were inveterate cholos, houses huddled in enclosed fields, submissive and quarrelsome chicha lovers, eccentric people chatting under the sun, and a good piece of land to live on, to grow on, because everything here was hallucination and dream, nobody eats, nobody dreams, like everyone is dead.

And so we bought clothes in La Cachina, I brought him to a public bathroom, we ate lunch, and he showed me his lodgings in zone two in a new settlement on the hill, four woven reed sides that an elderly woman rented to him in exchange for a plate of food. Once his needs were satisfied, Nakamatsu, as soon as he got to the roadway, without knowing why, or how, or when, turned inexorably toward the earthen streets, wooden hangars, blackened locksmith shops, firework stalls set up on patios, and countless buses, then descended from the settlement to the winding Tacora market amid a low hum. I never understood the reason for that brutal obsession, as if he wanted to expose himself to the indigents, the cholo hooligans, walking between piles of bolts, trowels, used clothes, old gadgets, obsolete chairs, and black vendors on their tricycle carts, and shampoo stools, and warped pots, and countless ratchets, nuts, pegs. There they were, the waves of sweaty people, with their fervid faces, their wrinkled outfits, in shirt-sleeves, their noses lethargic, legs stubborn, squabbling and haggling savagely. Then the unshakeable Katzuo, with that same meticulous-ness, went down Avenida México, on his way to the outskirts of San Jacinto, where the auto parts marketplace was, with its insolent men and lowlifes, offering crown wheels, examining gondolas, cylinders, chassis, and gearboxes, and exhaust pipes imposing in wooden huts, and plump mamacitas and child thieves. Katzuo concluded his apparently stubborn bewildered hours by measuring, weighing, solidly stunned, eyes unmoving, oblivious to the noises, focusing on emana-tions, gone astray in the air, as if nothing interested him, as if he was paying attention to nothing, or was disgorging himself, his past, his pride, his death, his life, as his imagination navigated the waters of emptiness, inhaling, exhaling. It was in that instant, in that suburb of San Jacinto, under the overpowering sun, that he started feeling the perverse stares behind him, the sobs, searing wails, insults, and a burst of screeching. And nevertheless, he did not want to twist around, or turn his head, or look, nothing, since it would be utterly useless, there wouldn't be anyone behind him, it was the wraiths, tumultuous shades that had always been after him, there they were unscathed, indolent, threatening, with their bountiful manes of hair, their blackened skin, scrofulous faces, and hard enlarged feet. He knew they were evil. Dreadful. The dark forces of destruction and death. It's possible they were vagrants, delinquents, rude unwholesome people, and perhaps Nakamatsu brushed shoulders with them, commingled with them, passing patient nighttime hours, indefinite time, because they weren't visible, nor would he have understood them, it was as if they were abstract animals, and there they were, caustic and malevolent.

For better or for worse, despite what was unforeseeable, Katzuo was fading, and felt as if his hours were numbered, perhaps he wanted to be swallowed, despoiled by the nothing. And so, without the felt hat now, he would perambulate through the streets with his shoulders thrown back, gestureless, his jacket unbuttoned, his pants discolored, beard unkempt, eyes abstruse and fixed on the sky, mind neutral, nothing to look at, nothing to feel. And it's possible that in the middle of this wreck, after sterile mornings and afternoons, possessed by hunger and fatigue, he would remember his arms, his legs, his name, and then, to calm his cravings, he would seek refuge in the stands in Parque Trompeteros, slowly consume a cup of oatmeal and an omelet, among jokesters and people eating on the go. And he, Katzuo, would sit there, legs crossed, hands on his thighs, oblivious to the sensation of cold in his stomach, dozing with his eyes open, listening to a distant whisper, an old Tuesday or Thursday exhaustion, like a film endlessly looped: the unencumbered Etsuko Untén in the years of the war, protesting when Prado's government expropriated Japanese-owned businesses, schools, properties, farms, and machinery. It was a terrible blow, they jailed managers, deported them, interrogated them, there were blacklists, extortions, robberies, spoliations, police on our heels, and the entire population hurling insults, degradations. Children were taken from their parents, families shamelessly and hungrily torn apart, running frightened, sheltering in their houses, uncomprehending. Katzuo saw them terrorized in the street, those infants, those women pleading, tearful, those Japanese people who went into hiding, others who fled to the sierra, jobless, unable to leave the house, because the neighbors threw rocks at us, we were the enemy, we were *nihonjin*, living a war we hadn't asked for.

As the tricycles went past on Nicolás Ayllón, which was sunny and then not, and in the distance the microbuses, the noise and conversations, Katzuo was not Katzuo, the hours were not hours, the people were not people, nor the animals, nor the rocks, nor the plates, the spoons, the tears, the pity, nothing existed, simply empty, no destination, no direction, no bitterness. In many ways, he, Katzuo, was nothing more than a rickety piece of furniture, spent, trembling, frightened by voices, presences, movements, boiling, dreaming of images that return, that pass by, totally shrunken, inert, body unmoving, sitting by any old stand, in any filthy old restaurant, elbows on the table, ankles crossed, forehead pacified, glasses having fallen off his nose, his stubble scruffy, grimy. And only after night had fallen, at nine, perhaps, or eleven, would he rise urgently from wherever he was, and with his erratic, irregular gait, as if he had pebbles in his shoes, he would make his way to dissolute Avenida Floral, that impertinent ramshackle avenue with its little rusting houses, where prostitutes, transsexuals, and young homosexuals stood leaning, shielded by the lampposts' dim light, and the food carts and the little windows of the stores. Immune to the air, the cold, the fear, Katzuo crossed the gas station goaded on by delight, approached the open lots, and stationed by the wall, there in the street, hallucinatory, he stared captivated at the homosexuals in the half light. As never before, as always, Katzuo felt a strange fascination, a mixture of fear and astonishment, his sensitivities exasperated, no control, chin rigid, and his hands quaked in his pants pockets. Despite the night air, and the presence of curious cars, and the arrival of spiteful passersby, and the boil of the unwholesome streets, Katzuo stayed put in his corner, spying, stalking, meandering, pallid and queasy, glimpsing manes of hair, trapping their smells, sensing their unyielding chests, decoding their skin, catching whiffs of their secretions, and then he was intoxicated, annoyed with himself, letting out sighs, his teeth grinding, releasing uncontrollable tears as he stood at the edge of the forbidden. Every night, every encounter, seemed different to him, implausible, his flesh sank into itself, his consciousness aroused, and he thought about nothing, as if he had reached the peak, and there were no longer wisps of strangeness, rootlessness, expatriation, extinction. And nevertheless, Nakamatsu knew, the sensation was elusive, fleeting, so he would have to return again and again to recover it, to swallow himself, without shame or bitterness, until sunrise, when the last homosexuals disappeared, and Katzuo returned to his ignominious condition of anguish, strolling around Avenida Circunvalación, the dusty breeze, the parallel streets, the hills' embankments, the dense parks and workshops, walking past the locksmiths, the stores selling doors, the tin tube vendors, and the dirty wheel shops, and the tricycle carts loaded with bottles. So much dismal humanity, dissolute chicha lovers, addicts, mestizos drinking in bars, trucks and mototaxis on the road. It's possible he remained unmoved in some hole in the wall, his coat unbuttoned, sweat on his forehead, shoes wheezing, vagrant, shoulders poised, smelling of goat, looking at no one, aloof, distant, absorbed in the air, in his exercise of inhaling and exhaling, and in the midst of so much persisting, so much disillusion and affliction, something definitive happened on just another nameless afternoon.

He was coming down Avenida Riva Agüero, after wandering past shanties and Parque San Cayetano, nothing foretold anything, the same idle streets, the same clutch of people, the same pernicious daytime radiation, when, for some unknown reason, he got to Nicolás Ayllón and, as he had so many times before, turned toward Mercado Virgen de la Asunción to examine the tiny tomatoes and fragrant onions. It might have been a sunny day, twelve or one in the afternoon; there was nothing in the unbreathable air, nothing in the rasping noises of the peddlers, when Katzuo, with his tattered shoes, his brittle gaze and darkened breathing, left behind the huge umbrellas and the burlap sack parapets. There they were, the masses of potatoes, heaps of olluco, smell of basil, eggplant freshness between iron scales. His curiosity piqued, he left behind the cauliflower and spilling cilantro, and without knowing why, he stopped in front of a steadfast young man in a blue shirt and jeans who was plucking rue leaves on a stool. He released a sigh when he saw that limpid olive complexion, then caught his breath before the Hagarite silhouette and those lips engraved in long sharp lines, the strange quizzical brows shadowing a dark, deep gaze, curling hair falling away from the face. In infinite time, Katzuo examined the young man's beautiful movements in the air, and only when he had finished sniffing at the admirable feet in their espadrilles did he let out a shriek that rang out across the entire market: it was a sob, a din emerging from his intestines, from the most secret parts of his unconscious. All those years later, after extraordinary searches, at the end of pressing insomnia and miserable days, finally he had found his shy young man with refined legs, perverse arms, pale lips, and a ring of inevitable teeth. The young man he had craved, longed for, dreamed of a thousand times, in infinite premonitions, on myriad squall-rocked nights. Immediately, Nakamatsu stripped off his jacket, shirt, pants, victorious shoes, and underwear, and was naked before the boy with the dark eyes, and the tightly packed crowd. Then, weeping, on his knees, crying out to heaven and hell, he simply whispered to himself: "Beauty does exist! Beauty does exist!" Katzuo Nakamatsu had achieved *kenshō*, *satori*, a vision of nature's essence.

9

W ITH THE CONSENT of family members, Katzuo Nakamatsu was admitted to the Social Security Psychiatric Institute and placed in pavilion two, in a white sun-soaked room. During the day, like all the patients, he was settled under the care of the nurses in a common room, where the patients could be entertained, hold a conversation, play games of chess or cards. Nevertheless, in his free time, Katzuo preferred sitting in a chair and observing the TV, though in reality he was looking for isolation, quiet and unmoving, staring at nothing, his eyes fixed on the screen, focusing on an abstract point, suspended in the atmosphere, exhaling and inhaling, no thoughts, no images, no memories, no emotions, nothing. It was his instinctive bearing, willingly free, exempt from everything, his eyes open, static, his consciousness purifying, his attention laboring, glacial and im-

mersed in himself, with a gesture of resignation, unwavering, uncapit-
ulating, like an inert stone or pot. And he could stay in that tenacious
position for hours, fighting with himself, absorbed and undistracted,
no roughness and no recourse, as he refused to accept any friendly
interruptions.

Naturally, Katzuo gradually recovered his faculties, bathing and shav-
ing every day, no more vagrant's habits, a man who complied with
the hospital schedule, under medical supervision, taking turns with
the other patients. Going down disquiet's strange paths, through the
turmoil of death, under the inclement wretchedness of sun and air,
without day or night, the body depraved, exhausted and attracted by
perversion, Katzuo had achieved *satori*. Stunned and bathed in tears,
sunk, in that moment, in beauty, his consciousness had seemed to leap
out of itself, bursting out and leaving the body, and then his mind had
been illumed as if plunged into the impervious force of the absolute.
And there had been no death, no cause, no emptiness, no abysmal
fears, no reason, no life, no expiration, no extinctions, all the dualities,
the contradictions settled themselves, were united, and then went
back to their never-ending battles. He well knew, Katzuo, that this
wasn't happiness or paradise, in that deliberate and tranquil way it
all had to be verified, his readjustment to equanimity, inner peace,
and bodily well-being. Even so, a natural order was possible within
the chaos, the urges, the inexorable inferno, and the strokes of bad

luck. That was all. After his gradual recuperation: the return to the everyday of always, that which belonged to Katzuo himself and his genial educated man's certainty, his walks through the city, his friends in Parque El Porvenir, his weighty research, and the writing of his novels, which would now occur from within his immeasurable vision and the unexpected flashes of his enlightenment.

Outwardly, everything was going smoothly, the visits from family, the psychiatric consultations, Katzuo tidy and meticulous, integrated with the community in the hospital. Except for those tortuous early mornings, when everything seemed to contort and spin out of control, because that was when his sleeping body, trapped by a strange phosphorescence, devolved into inflamed crisis, and stopped obeying him, convulsing, quivering in miry visions. In his little room, at that unusual hour, Katzuo would wake up wild and furious, his eyes violent, hands shaking and legs uncontrolled, his face pallid, grimacing, spewing babble, scandalous shouting, and garbled stuttering. The night nurses would appear, and facing that din and disarray, they squeezed him into a straitjacket, gagged him, and injected him with a powerful sleeping aid. He would stay this way until the next day, when we would find him diluted, sitting at the edge of the bed, quiet and perfectly groomed, his face mild, hands docile, and skin unperturbed, ready for his walk in the main room, with the other residents, murmuring his nostalgia, "Like one smooth oil against two vinegars." In these circumstances, as on other occasions, one of his relatives hinted that the only person who could bring him out of his predicament was the inestimable Juan Miyazaki, owner of the restaurant Midori on Plaza Ruiz Gallo in Lince. They'd known each other since they were children, and were about the same age, with the same ways of thinking, even the same reactions, and so once Juan Miyazaki was notified, he wasted no time in coming. He arrived one Sunday during visiting hours, in a navy jacket and neat tie, his whiskers in place and his expressions discreet, evidently aware of his importance, such that they arranged for the meeting to take place in the reception hall. No words passed between them, nor signs of softening, nor prior circumlocutions, Juan Miyazaki, faithful to his peaceable habits, simply gave him a glass of rum and a pack of cigarettes, and Katzuo Nakamatsu contained his surprise, and all he did was sip the rum, and chain-smoke two cigarettes. Nothing more was required. Sitting face to face, no spectators, looking into each other's eyes, making calculations in the silence, attuned to each breath, each flicker of the face, inhaling shared smells, studying the gleams in each other's skin, reciprocally excavating their guts, moving on to legs, kidneys, livers, intestinal secretions. Only when he had finished his exhaustive inspection did Juan Miyazaki grab his troubled forehead, and in a choked voice he managed to say:

"Miyagui *yuta!*"

~

In the days that followed, we went looking via Katzuo's family members for the *yuta* Miyagui, an Okinawan medium skilled in tracking the emanations of dead souls and the needs of bodiless beings through the churn of her sensitivity. She was small and chubby, with a wrinkled face, a head of ash-colored hair, and broad coarse-knuckled hands, and she moved around unsteadily in the mystery of her eighty years. And nevertheless she was obliging, inquisitive, and warm, fumbling through an acceptable Japanese-Spanish, and seemed to be good-natured, with a steely tenacity in her eyes. She took over Nakamatsu's room, and gently, slowly, and earnestly, she sprinkled the floor with salt, then burned incense in all the corners, moved the bed to the sunrise position, and later sat down in an armchair to wait, it seemed her best qualities were patience and composure, while she reached for her twilight visions. She made no ostentatious gestures, but her angular gaze examined the room beyond the unflappable Katzuo, recording in her mind the insignificant objects, making out colors, apparent details, saying nothing, tireless and unfaltering, trusting in her inspiration to corner wilted spirits, and receive messages from death's province. She had no recourse but to wait the whole day, maintaining her splendid stoicism the next morning and the following evening, and only on the third day, at dawn, sleepless, having kept vigil all night, already harboring her suspicions, engrossed, did she witness the shape of Nakamatsu's crisis. When she saw him collapsed on the floor, agitated and quivering, writhing as he trembled, his legs and arms shaking, rocking and roaring horribly, the *yuta* Miyagui asked for the windows and doors to be shut and the light turned off. In that complete darkness, amid the bellowing, she approached the disturbed body, and felt his fever and his most intimate substance, with no other recourse, she saw Katzuo's evanescent aura emerge, a yellow gleam, and then a flash of light. The *yuta* Miyagui, straining to focus, gathering all her strength, all her might, all her drive, saw foliage, inflamed greenery, and the leaves of a thicket; then she perceived the vibration of birds, the murmur of a waterfall, and a temperate wind blowing through bamboo groves, and greedy creeks. Above the scene and the slope, near the bluish sky, was a clear spilling spring, and beyond that circled something like buzzing, whispering, and hoarse rattling: those sounds came from the distance, from somewhere far away, from a remote and completed past. They were yesterday's murmurs, multiplied in flights of fancy, men and women in a horde, or rather a mob of Japanese who did not falter, exerting themselves on a land that wasn't theirs, dripping sweat and tears, old specters from Katzuo's childhood, appearing, humiliated, bursting forth here and there, irreversible, furious, deranged, in an insoluble rush. And from among all the coos and growls, and the many ghosts, according to the *yuta* Miyagui, arose a panting voice, stifled and gnarled, imposing itself, rasping, in a torrent: "That friend of your father's, Etsuko Untén, did not return to Lima in vain. He, the former tramp, a bumpkin without a cent in his pocket, put on a hat, a vest, English trousers, and suede shoes, to show everyone that you can never lose your race or your pride. Even during the war, when Prado's government came after us and confiscated our property, Etsuko Untén would stroll around Quinta Heeren, a haughty provocateur, looking people in the face, withstanding countless insults. And he would attend the Church of Our Lady of Cocharcas, to face his lot, defiant and unwilling to acquiesce, rounding the Palacio de Gobierno, so everyone could see that we would never be defeated, not by Roosevelt, not by the Allied Forces. *Nihon* couldn't possibly lose the war, we had known only eternal victory, we had never surrendered, despite living as captives in an enemy country, among preposterous whites and scatterbrained cholos. In those days, Etsuko Untén had begun to establish gathering places for *kachigumi*, in Barrios Altos, in Rimac, in Breña, to provide services for poor Japanese, those who had been left without work, at the mercy of a people who despised and rejected us. Don't forget, all the attacks and humiliations we experienced, any old person could threaten us like we were pariahs: your father Zentaró had his little grocery snatched away. Nagamine *ojisan* was extorted by two policemen, who tried to take his daughters under the pretext of the war, and he could do nothing but die of shame because he couldn't go into the street. Every criollo, every thug, robbed us and exploited us even in our misfortune. Irey-*san* was put in jail and deported to the United States for being the teacher at the Japanese school, and his wife and children went with him. We were in the palm of their hands, our en-

emies, accused of being fifth columnists, and imprisoned by the rage
of the people, the rabble-rousers, the political meddlers, the riffraff,
the looters, and the general malevolence."

That elusive, unsettled voice, according to the *yuta* Miyagui, belonged
to a woman who, from memory's rubble, stretched effulgent over
Nakamatsu's trembling body, as if she had crossed troubled waters,
sterile deserts, and ravines swollen with rancor. At times she gasped,
furious, strangled by explosions and rebukes, opening herself in a torrent onto rocks and earth scorched by acrimony: "Keep in mind how
we were knocked down, the government and the country against us,
exploited by hostile people, who wanted to set up San Lorenzo Island
to house us there on behalf of American interests, that's what they
said. Or, otherwise, send us to the jungle, to inhospitable settlements,
as prisoners of war, another thing they said. And all the while, we
were willing to face our lots as *nihonjin*, as a race, as a people, because
the vicissitudes of life had us living here, in this inhospitable land,
surrounded by thieves. And oh, the paradoxes of history, never forget,
we had to deal with the vindictiveness of the Chinese colony, since in
the moiling river of events, whenever they could, they would report
us to the authorities. They put up Chinese flags at their properties
and businesses so they wouldn't be confused for Japanese, and during
the public frenzy they tried to save their own hides. And they knew
us, they knew who we were, our schools and newspapers, and the

configurations of our groups, that's how they became informers for the investigating commissions and American intelligence services. In San Nicolás, in Supe, in Chancay, Paramonga, or Cañete, in Pisco, in Arequipa, in the districts and hamlets of Trujillo, or in Chiclayo, in every province and on every hacienda, wherever a census was taken, they gave us away, ruthlessly. Understand this, they could never forgive us, they were Chinese raising their Kuomintang flags, supporters of Chiang Kai-shek, we were at war, and Japan had occupied Manchuria, and we had colonized numerous cities across the continent. These were old grudges, whether or not we knew it, the way Etsuko Untén and the *kachigumi* knew it, unwilling to be trampled, folding into themselves to defend this scrap of pride that will not capitulate, this shred of dignity that refuses to submit. That's why Etsuko Untén would go out into the public plaza, puffed with pride, passionate in his delirium, unshakeable in his purpose, confronting his enemies while utterly exposed, cunning and dark, his smile contemptuous, his greetings refined, striding forward without bitterness, knowing full well he could be lynched, suicidal and looking, perhaps, for death.

"By that time, we were hoping for the news that would later make the rounds, according to which the imperial majesty was sending a ship to pick up all the Japanese in Peru, so we could make our way back to the eternal fatherland, so we could convey to the four winds that we had not given up. On the other hand, Etsuko Untén, it's true, was not accepted by his fellow countrymen. He was despised and attacked, since they considered him *kichigai*, crazy, shameless, rash, and *baka*, stupid, idiotic, and that's why many people turned their backs on him, since his zealous emotions and uncouth style as he demanded weapons and explosives provoked astonishment and fear, and nobody trusted him, blinded as he was by his battle and grappling with himself. All he had was a handful of *kachigumi*, nationalists clinging to tradition, intimately willing to strap on their armor, inured to passions running high and the din of the struggle. And so, following the heart's plans, galvanized by the somber retreat, with no gear, no bullets, no firearms, we had to face up to everyone on our own, and provide an answer to the people humiliating us, and a city that loathed us. That was when we built the house, the charter for that indestructible Japanese house, to serve as a safe haven, meeting place, shelter for those who had been disowned, for the Japanese without jobs, for families shattered and undone, for those with a hunger and thirst for revenge. And we built it with the best of ourselves, in the heart of La Victoria, on the distant Calle Francia, far from the noise, in three months of work, with lacquered wood, *kuromatsu* pilings, sliding doors, kakemonos, and many flourishes, including a clever waterfall, nestled rocks, green gardens, ornamental fish, and a bamboo grove. Those who came were people who had lost everything, and who needed to make amends, and together they assembled screens, fitted together stairs, and with modest simplicity, in the middle of that war, the elegant varnished house, with its two floors, its three tiled eaves, its passageways, the main altar, the rooms with their *tatami*, the resin floors, and the beloved flag of the *nihonjin* fluttering at the entrance, looked like a beautiful animal of resistance that satisfied our yearning for longevity. It was the place we had foreseen, the object of our stirred-up feelings, with a somber Etsuko Untén pacing in the gardens, meticulously dressed in a vest, hat, gabardine trousers, and suede shoes, to face his lot, something he considered a matter of honor. And we had the *obāsan* feeding the children, and the *ojiisan* consoling those who'd been stripped of their land, businesses, and fields, about the slander; it was like a palliative for our despair, and it was from there, that fortified territory we considered our own soil, that letters were written and messages dispatched, we joined our strength together, listened to the NHK, and followed the news from the war in the Pacific, interspersed between marches and glorious anthems. We couldn't backtrack, not for suspicion, not for abuse, said Yonashiro-*san*, and it was repeated by Hajime *niisan*, we hoped for the triumph of the *nihonjin* over the Allied Forces, even when we were captive in enemy territory, enduring countless ambushes, alert to police raids and political groups; don't forget the racial animosity, and the criollos who never wanted us here. And one and all, they organized searches and police visits, cheered reports about us, attended rallies and shows of force, and we were only able to last six months, until one morning in March of 1943, when a mob of fanatics, arrayed into shock troops, forced their way into the house and torched the facilities, swept along by political furor, Peruvian flags, and bellicose rancor. They set fire to the eaves, destroyed the waterfalls, accusing us of being invaders building up an army, they reduced everything to ruins, leaving no plank of wood untouched, they even pulled out the *leake* shrubs and the dovecote, burning everything, flames multiplying, and the dense black smoke could be seen from Plaza Manco Cápac."

That harried voice, loaded full of sobs, outbursts, and indignation, shifted around tirelessly. The accent was that of a *nēsan*, an old *nisei* woman left marked by the horrors, and according to the *yuta* Miyagui, she was fixated on Katzuo because he was the son of Zentaró, Etsuko Untén's friend. Perhaps Katzuo Nakamatsu had heard that accent in his childhood, which had been tormented and laden with ghosts, and it was possible he had been shown the tense and stony face of that *nesan*, among the many faces in the familial and domestic realm, simply so he would not forget the arduous humiliations of those Japanese people. And the same voices and apparitions arrived back at his consciousness, and retreated into themselves there, alive, in the abyss of the past, like a derisive shout, tossing and swirling in pride's swamp over spite and intractable resentments. But Nakamatsu, lying on the floor, in that hospital room, drowning in convulsions, looked like an inert and slackened body unresponsive to vital urges, and it was the *yuta* Miyagui who held him up and helped him with her twilight energies. In any case, the voice whip-cracked between mirages and came back around again and again, impetuous and tenacious: "There was nothing left of that house. People were detained, injured, killed, and brought to trial. Etsuko Untén came out miraculously untouched, and had to seek refuge in the cotton fields of Comuco, protected by Japanese families that were able to conceal him. Despite the devastation, he, inexorable, fatal, would not turn back, he was still able to gather together the last of his belongings, and his will stricken, he moved on to Callao to fight his final battle. Perhaps he didn't see it that way, but in those difficult times, poor and rejected by his countrymen, who blamed him for those violent events, pursued and cornered by those unworthy of trust, he ended up on a street near the docks, where he lived in a rustic shack owned by Okinawans. He was never as much himself as he was then. People were trying to kill him, and nevertheless, every morning and every afternoon, always wearing his unchanging hat, his bowtie, impeccable pants, and suede shoes, he stood firm on the Callao pier or sat in some little plaza facing the sea, among rickety boats and cormorants, to stare eagerly at the horizon, looking for the inevitable ship coming to pick up the Japanese moored in Peru. No agonizing, no commotion, no defeat, Etsuko Untén, don't forget, had no reason to stop believing, to doubt that that ship would pull into port, in his absolute conviction, in his ironclad dignity, in his eternal invincible defense of *Nihon*. They called him crazy, *bakatare*, idiot, he was humiliated a thousand times over, his own countrymen turned their backs on him, but he continued waiting, obdurate and incorruptible, because he considered it a matter of honor, outside of time, of the vicissitudes of history, of life's little circumstances, even after the setback in Hiroshima and Japan's unconditional surrender. Never forget, Etsuko Untén refused to capitulate. Every morning and every afternoon, he must have dressed himself to go to the port, to wait, even in his old age, to sit in a park, alone and melancholy, attuned to the sea, his gaze lost to that mythical ship that would arrive at the coast, so we could keep fighting for a country that had long forgotten us. And even in 1956, the aged Etsuko Untén was still going up and down the docks, crossing paths with fishermen and stevedores, next to the barges and that immense sea, in his wilted outfit, his skin worn, and his smile impenetrable, with an inkling that the ship would berth at the wharf, he was steadfast, waiting with no other recourse, no illusions, unfathomable, crazy, dark and enigmatic. And only when he was certain that death would reach him before the ship did, in his peaceable dying moments, he finally settled into a posture of abandonment, in that plaza, in that park, sitting there, facing the sea, that is, symptomatically speaking, he bowed his head, placed his hands on his thighs, and palmed his slack legs, which no longer contained any desire to live."

That turbulent morning, this was the testimony given by the *yuta* Miyagui above the bleak and plaintive body of Katzuo Nakamatsu.

In the days that followed, it was Katzuo who took his tranquil stroll around the salon, chatting and playing cards with the other patients. He moved around, no marks or signs, benign, his immutable face, patient in his conversations, his gestures polite, his voice always low, cheerful, refined, like nothing had happened, as if his many masks and countless layered veils hid the intricate wounds in his consciousness. Later, he returned to his house on extension La Mar in El Porvenir to continue with his normal activities, always with the same propriety, the same deliberate movement of arms and legs during his strolls, and the same ambiguous, neutral expression we had always known. For the present text, he was kind enough to send me his studies on Japanese families, and files and notes about his parents; I was also able to read his unfinished novel and collate his personal diaries. Two months after leaving the hospital, Katzuo Nakamatsu died of a sudden brain aneurysm.

Afterword

Three days after I arrived in Lima for a Fulbright fellowship in August 2019, I purchased my first shrink-wrapped copy of the second edition of *La iluminación de Katzuo Nakamatsu*—the translation of which you now hold in your hands. Published in 2015 by the Asociación Peruano Japonesa (Japanese Peruvian Association), the second edition has a cover featuring an illustration of a male figure facing away from the viewer, and a section of black-and-white photos at the back titled "Higa, el iluminado" (Higa, the enlightened).

Among the photos is a series of the author; the caption notes that these portraits were taken for the first edition of Augusto's 1977 story collection *Que te coma el tigre* (Let the tiger eat you). Augusto, who must have been in his early 30s, is wearing dark plastic frames, and his hair is about shoulder length. There's one shot in particular I love because it feels dynamic and surprising. In it, Augusto's face is tilted up, mouth open in a shout or a laugh. His hand is in the foreground, but it's overexposed, so I can't tell if he's pointing at us or making a fist. Another image in the black-and-white dossier is a reproduction of the front of the 2008 first edition of this novel. I was struck by the older cover, which is centered on what looks to be a laughing okame / otafuku mask emerging out of a dark background—eerie and evocative of the specters that come to haunt Katzuo.

A week and a half after I bought the copy of *La iluminación de Katzuo Nakamatsu* I still use now, I made my way to the lovely Librería Escena Libre on the recommendation of Sebastian, a limeño friend of a friend who had graciously sat with me one afternoon in Iowa City and suggested a list of places to check out. The proprietor of Escena Libre, Julio, is a fount of literary knowledge. I purchased all the Augusto Higa Oshiro books he had in stock, as well as a thick stack of other books he recommended. Given that the movement of books between the US and Latin American literary hubs beyond Mexico City and Buenos Aires is generally not free-flowing, part of my mission for my time in Lima was to collect as many interesting works as possible, both references and books that were new to me.

After expressing my interest in Higa Oshiro's work to a couple of friends in Lima, one afternoon I found myself standing in front of a wide wooden gate. When the door within the gate popped open, I walked across the front yard and was greeted by a small dog and

Augusto. We sat down to chat. Augusto speaks deliberately, unhurriedly. He mentioned he was working toward a master's in literature and writing a thesis on the influential Peruvian writer Julio Ramón Ribeyro. We talked about all the books he was reading. I mentioned I was translating his story "Corazón sencillo" ("Simple Heart"), and he smiled and explained where the story had come from: he had been inspired by Ryunosuke Akutagawa's "Sennin" and Gustave Flaubert's "Un cœur simple" ("A Simple Heart"), whose title morphed into that of his own story. He listened to me describe an issue of *Words Without Borders* I was guest-editing and then shared that his story "Okinawa existe," ("Okinawa exists") from his third collection of the same name, had taken flight from Chinese Peruvian writer Siu Kam Wen's short story "El tramo final" ("The Final Stretch"). At one point he ducked into the study off the living room and returned with a volume of scholarship about his work, which he gave to me.

By that point, I was vaguely aware of what I now know well, which is that there are (thus far) two phases to Augusto's literary career. The story collection *Que te coma el tigre* was his first book and is emblematic of the first phase, in which his fiction rarely moved outside the neighborhoods of his childhood in Lima's working-class historic center. As he said in a 2009 interview, speaking for Grupo Narración, the group of writers he was affiliated with: "We wanted to create a language of the people, of the coast, the city, the urban center, the gangs, or the underworld."

In the early 1990s, Higa spent a year and a half as a dekasegi doing factory work in Japan. His subsequent return to Peru marked the beginning of the second phase. In 1994, he published a memoir recounting his disorienting stint in Japan, titled *Japón no da dos oportunidades* (Japan doesn't give second chances). Next came *La iluminación de Katzuo Nakamatsu*, followed by the story collection *Okinawa existe* and the novel *Gaijin* (Japanese for "foreigner"). The nikkei characters and stories that had been invisible in his early works arrived in full force. "Those types of stories hadn't come easily," he said in a 2014 interview, "because I didn't know how to create them. Only after forty years do they come out with ease. Because I finally managed to demarcate that world."

One aspect of Augusto's work that remains unchanged between his two phases is his attention to the texture of language. In his introduction to a 2014 compendium of all his short fiction, Augusto writes: "to make for effective storytelling, a particular type of language was needed, language that was capable of imposing itself on the breath."

"Breathless" is a word that often occurred to me when I was in the thick of translating *The Enlightenment of Katzuo Nakamatsu*. Augusto's sentences in this novel are elliptical, often anaphoric, building to a swaying rhythm that slips by like silk and is likewise slippery to pin down in a new language. When I translate poetry, the sensation is something akin to bringing the page very close to my face so I can look extra hard at the words, and I often had that feeling when translating this novel, even though it is not, technically, poetry. But looking closely and fixedly at this novel left me more breathless than translating poetic language usually does, I think because the units of verse poetry are generally shorter, and that sort of tight attention is easier to sustain for smaller units—the enjambed line versus the tumbling sentence testing its virgular bounds, the poem versus the chapter.

The physical experience of translating the final chapter was different from the rest of the manuscript. I wrote a first draft in a vibrating headlong push, swept along by the forceful torrents of words that make up much of the chapter. Occasionally, I would look up and realize I was more hunched into myself than usual, muscles kinked into positions that strained, and I would consciously work to unknot everything, lower my shoulders from their place by my earlobes, ripple fingers that had started to feel like claws. My back was especially achy during that stretch of days. I remembered essays by other translators that trace the physical effects of their work—Lara Vergnaud on translating Franck Bouysse's *Of No Woman Born* and Ahmed Bouanani's *The Hospital*, Laura Marris on translating Albert Camus's *The Plague*.

I recognized what Lara Vergnaud calls "Movement as a vehicle to find language" from my own habits as a translator. In an essay for *Words Without Borders*, Vergnaud describes "connecting with a text on a sensory level . . . I would hunch my shoulder, mimicking a mother pushing her arm through the neck of a nightgown to breastfeed her child; tap one finger in the air, imagining myself a smoker sending a rain of cigarette ashes into his palm." I had found my hands moving as I envisioned scenes in my head—Katzuo crocheting, Katzuo lifting a pistol to his temple—and I wondered whether my hunching over the final chapter was an echo of Katzuo's posture as he was buffeted by otherworldly monologues. By the time I finished that first draft of the last chapter, I felt drained, my head echoing with someone else's caustic emotion that felt both familiar and fresh. But the process of revision, always my favorite part of the translation process, delivered me back to Katzuo's familiar vacillating gait. Retracing his descent into enlightenment gradually refilled me with lightness and delight.

The way Augusto so directly named his influences to me is a reminder that making a text is never a solitary endeavor, even if it sometimes feels like it. I am grateful to Ignacio López-Calvo and his book *The Affinity of the Eye: Writing Nikkei in Peru*, which is how I first learned of Augusto. I am grateful for the support from Cornell University's Institute for Comparative Modernities. I am grateful to the editors at Archipelago and to all the friends and fellow translators whose eyes have passed over these pages and made them better (AA, MA, DB, HC, DM, EG, HG, EH, SH, LHK, KK, CM, GM, GRC, JS, KS, MW, among others). I am grateful for Diego's work on Augusto's behalf to make this book possible. And I am grateful to you, reader, for coming into these pages with me.

Jennifer Shyue, 2023

archipelago books

is a not-for-profit literary press devoted to
promoting cross-cultural exchange through innovative
classic and contemporary international literature
www.archipelagobooks.org